About the author

Born in Shanghai in 1976, Yue Tao has lived in Amsterdam since 2000. With a B.A. in English language and literature from Fudan University in Shanghai and an M.A. in Social Sciences (cum laude) from the University of Amsterdam, she is a business storyteller, intercultural trainer, and freelance essayist whose articles appear in English and Chinese newspapers, magazines, and multimedia. She hosted live broadcasts from Chinese Radio Amsterdam and the sex, art, and literature forum at the Amsterdam China Festival.

Shanghai Blue is her debut novel. The Chinese original *Hong xishuai* 'Red Cricket' appeared in June 2012 and the Dutch translation *Schemering boven Shanghai* in January 2015. She is completing a sequel set in the Netherlands.

Shanghai Blue

FSC
www.fsc.org
MIX
Papier van
verantwoorde herkomst
FSC® C004472

Yue Tao

Shanghai Blue

World Editions

Published in Great Britain in 2015 by World Editions Ltd., London

www.worldeditions.org

Cover design Multitude
Image credit © Wenjie Yang/MoST

First published as *Hong xishuai* by Huacheng Chubanshe

British Library Cataloguing-in-Publication Data
A catalogue record for this book is available on request from the British Library

ISBN 978-94-6238-001-1

Typeset in Minion Pro

Distribution Europe (except the Netherlands and Belgium):
Turnaround Publisher Services, London
Distribution the Netherlands and Belgium: Centraal Boekhuis, Culemborg, the Netherlands

To my husband and son

Contents

Prologue

Dazzled by the white sunlight of European summer, I sit on a playground bench and watch Adam shoveling in a sandbox. The sound of sand falling into his bucket resonates the rustle of tree leaves in the breeze. He knits his little brow, totally absorbed as if building a monument. His features are exquisite. I stare enraptured, unable to believe he is mine.

I am grateful almost to tears: contemplation of absolute tranquility piques the will to believe in Providence. But that night three years ago obtrudes—surreptitious attraction on an evening out, hot adultery in the dark, warm skin on cold sheets, ghostly reflections in the wardrobe mirror …

People often ask what brought me back to Amsterdam. I say a letter—a letter that made me leave Shanghai. They think I must be a political refugee; I neither confirm nor deny their presumption. Is my situation any better? A refugee who escapes is free but no matter how far away I get, what happened that night holds me spellbound.

Only I know the facts—the letter is ashes, the cousin who wrote it is dead; as long as I say nothing, the events never happened.

I thought burning the letter would free me but as it shriveled away page by page, my horror, shame, and guilt clung—and still cling a continent away in this deceptively simple, quiet country. They irrupt without warning when I am happiest.

I fled my partner in crime but cannot escape the memory. I am locked in a mental prison where I am both inmate and guard. Possessed by that unspeakable sin, I must be my own exorcist and free my soul by recounting my experience as it happened—in the present tense. I see no other way to consign it to oblivion.

Homecoming

1

Shanghai smells of mildew. Muggy air assaults as I step off the plane. I remember only the monsoon season having this smell. Now it is August, a month after the monsoon, but the smell is everywhere—passport control, luggage hall, people's clothes, taxi seats … The city reeks of decay. Everything in it rots—even modern, glittery, chic young men and women.

This familiar smell upsets and soothes me. My mind says my hometown should be clean, bright, fashionable, modern, proud. But my senses tell me it is not: I smell the walls of my childhood home in the monsoon season—walls that sweated gray-green mildew spots and stank of wet plaster.

I arrive at midnight on 7 August. Wishing not to disturb my elderly aunt and uncle, I told them I would arrive the next morning. Tonight I stay downtown at the South Ocean Hotel. After checking in, settling into the room, and taking a bath, I feel no urge to sleep and go downstairs to the bar.

This bar called Mask is more popular than the hotel itself. Most customers are not hotel guests. In summer the garden is open. I choose a table beside a tree and order a glass of white wine. The night air is summer sticky and smells of dark green plants. A breeze now and then lightens the air, making the humidity bearable.

Crickets chirp shrilly in the bushes. I cannot remember how long ago I last heard them—ten years at least. I came home several times to visit meanwhile but somehow missed this season. I cannot even remember hearing crickets since I grew up. Too busy? Too distracted? Crickets chirping recall the long uneventful autumn nights of my childhood. I thought these little creatures might go extinct, but they endure as if to remind me I am home for good.

Candlelight reflects in the sunglasses of a man at the table opposite. I have been studying him. His lion nose and peach-flower mouth, which make his face at once harsh and gentle, are familiar. He seems to be observing me as well though I cannot tell for sure—I cannot see his eyes. Why wear sunglasses at night? He is sitting under a lamp; insects dance above his head, but he seems not to mind or even notice. He wears a silk shirt; the light gives it a distorted purple color. The collar is open; around his neck is a red string, probably suspending a jade talisman. He looks about forty, a businessman—maybe a restaurant owner or seafood dealer. Did I meet him somewhere?

As I rack my brain guessing who he might be he stands up, swills the rest of his drink, and walks away. I stop guessing. If I really know him the name will come back when I am not thinking about it. Most likely I do not know him at all—he could be just a passerby from years ago.

A loud motor howls, a scarlet Lamborghini pulls away, the man in sunglasses at the wheel. The rear license plate reads: Shanghai A-88888. Above the number it says: FUK U.

Damn jet lag! I oversleep. I promised my aunt I would arrive in the morning but get there at one in the afternoon. My aunt and uncle are waiting for me. An untouched banquet covers the dining table—pork marinated in salt and rice wine, fried river fish stewed in soy sauce, fried tomatoes and zucchini, cucumber salad in vinegar, plus a pork chop and winter melon soup.

They always treat me like their own child—they are one reason I decided to come home to Shanghai from Amsterdam. They are healthy but well into their seventies with nobody to take care of them. Two years ago on a visit I hired a countrywoman to clean house, shop, and cook for them, but they soon let her go. 'We are not used to food cooked by other people,' they said, but in fact did not want me to waste money. When I worked at the bank in Amsterdam my salary was generous by Chinese standards. Frugal their whole life they find my expenditures painfully exorbitant.

My aunt is tender and solicitous. She loves and cares for me, and sometimes I feel she loves me even more than her daughter, my cousin. My uncle is kind and quiet. Wearing thick glasses, he bent for years over a desk stacked with papers. His back is now hunched. As a child I was proud of them because they were trilingual in Chinese, Korean, and Vietnamese. They were translators for the factory they worked at and met in Vietnam when sent there to learn the language. Retired twenty years now they stay home with nothing to do—every day is aimless but comfortable and relaxing.

After lunch my uncle slices a watermelon.

'I can't eat another bite,' I say.

'Today autumn begins,' he replies. 'Eating watermelon is our custom.'

I have no idea how the custom originated. Perhaps when autumn begins watermelons get scarce so one must eat them quickly. It was only while abroad that I discovered how ignorant I am of tradition, as if my first twenty-two years of life were wasted.

I went abroad ten years ago, first to study for two years, then to work at a multinational bank. My job from a Chinese point of view was a golden rice bowl whereas to me it was golden handcuffs—nice to see but not to wear. In the eight years I worked at the bank I was promoted only once: the new task differed little from the old and the pay raise was negligible. I tried to change jobs several times but the new offers were worse and I soon got too lazy to keep looking. Sitting on a permanent contract, I did the same thing day after day. Often, watching my youth slip away, I was seized with panic—I saw death pressing closer and closer. One day I decided to go home and start a new life. I had nothing to lose but a boring job—no property, no family, no steady boyfriend. To me it meant no burden though most Chinese would consider it proof of failure.

'Are your classmates all married now?' my aunt asks.

'Some are, some aren't.'

'Do the married ones have children?'

'Some do, some don't.'

My one hesitation about coming home is my aunt's penchant for matchmaking. Her discipline was always strict: I was forbidden boyfriends and had to be home by nine at night. The day I graduated from university, however, she started matchmaking. Then I went abroad. Too far away for micro-management, she switched to telephone consultancy. International phone calls were expensive but not enough to stop her: 'I met an old colleague today who asked if you're married and have a child …' I got annoyed once and said, 'If anyone asks again you give her eight words—*no girl marry out, no child come out!*' She spoke no more about it after that. I felt guilty but did not want to say so, fearing she might start up again. Now she knows I am home to settle down. Her matchmaking passion rekindles.

'The other day I ran into an old colleague who asked after you.'

'Any news of my cousin?' I redirect evasively.

'How could we have any news?' my uncle replies. 'The police said last week they hadn't found her in ten years and therefore closed the case.'

'You mean that's it?'

'What else could we do? The police said it's 99 percent certain she's dead.'

This no-news news makes me forget about matchmaking. We all guessed she was dead, but the announcement shocks me.

She was their only child, fifteen years older than I. Paralyzed with polio at three, she was confined to a wheelchair. Her lower body was no bigger than a child's, making her head and upper body look outsize. I remember her sequestered in her tiny room with an almost lightless view to the north, emerging only to heat water in the kitchen to wash her hair. I do not know why she liked washing her hair so much; maybe it was because she thought her shiny black hair was the one part of her body she could be proud of. My aunt and uncle always told me not to disturb her, saying she was preparing for the university entrance exams. She was always preparing for the exams but never passed. The year I went to junior high she gave up and worked at the local community council as a telephone operator. Once every household got a private phone she took small fees from illiterate Party members to ghostwrite reports they had to submit on what they thought about policy decrees. Shortly after I went abroad she went missing.

She and I were not close, but she taught me the good habit of reading. At age seven I read film magazines with her; at age nine, supermarket romances; at age eleven, travel adventures. In junior high I finished her World Classics collection. In senior high I lost interest in her books and bought my own.

Maybe because I liked reading I was good at school, which I hated. School made me anxious; I still feel the chill. I looked forward to vacation and growing up. But looking forward slows time—vacation always seemed to recede and growing up never to happen. Now, in no time, I am over thirty. This transformation was so quiet and seamless that I failed to notice it—like my cousin's disappearance and death.

2

I was born the day of Chairman Mao's funeral—18 September 1976. The wailing of millions, my aunt said, drowned out my feline cries. Everyone was weeping. The sobs betrayed grief, fear, relief, and worry. A new life came into the world as funeral music blared from loudspeakers throughout the city. That year people's eardrums went numb from funeral music. It was a year of mourning—for three founding fathers of the People's Republic and for hundreds of thousands killed by the great earthquake. They called me Lan—Blue—hoping I would have a tranquil mind, placid like the blue sky.

I spent my first twelve years in a southwest Shanghai suburb called 'countryside' in dialect. It had twenty-four apartment buildings, three abreast in eight rows. Due north was the main road beyond which stood the factory where my aunt and uncle worked. West was another paved road beyond which farm fields stretched off into the distance. East was a river beyond which endless farm fields also stretched. South was a small muddy road. Every morning and evening watchful farmers squatted beside it with plastic basins, sieves, and shoes piled up at their feet, asking passersby if they had ration coupons for cigarettes. The farmers bartered their goods for coupons to resell at a profit to cigarette addicts. When they saw policemen coming they packed up and dispersed in no time.

My aunt and uncle worked for that factory from the day

they were assigned there upon leaving school till the day they retired. The factory had a name, but everyone called it 416. My uncle said it was a code number—the government gave all military factories a code number. When my aunt and uncle talked about former schoolmates they also used code names: Old K worked at 409, Young K worked at 578, and so on.

Every morning at eight sharp military music blared from the factory loudspeaker. Still chewing their last mouthful of breakfast, workers emerged from the twenty-four buildings and bustled toward the factory gate. At twelve sharp the same music blared and workers from all factory departments streamed toward the dining hall. Those with schoolchildren or old parents living in went home to cook. Employees returned to their workstations at one and, exchanging rumors and gossip, waited for military music to blare at five. And so it went day in day out year after year. Over time the twenty-four buildings were repainted from gray to brown, brown to yellow, and back to gray again.

There were two schools for workers' children—Guangyuan Elementary School and Guangyuan Middle School. Children from the twenty-four buildings felt superior to children from the surrounding farm communities: they spoke accentless Shanghai dialect and knew they did not have peasants for parents. They wore key chains around their necks and when school let out at three they played outdoors like feral cats, but never with farm children from the villages. In summer they walked twenty minutes in scorching heat to the nearby university pool rather than swim in the river with them.

In those years of scarcity children were happy. Any piece of junk, any captive vermin, any abnormal person brought joy. They enjoyed harassing Loony Lulu, a lunatic in the building next to the one where my aunt and uncle lived. I never knew when Lulu went insane; I just remember her standing at the front window repeating the same sentence: 'I'll wait for you by the river tonight.' In the spring they threw moth eggs at her; in the summer, caterpillars; in the fall, toads; in the winter, firecrackers. She always closed the window quietly, pressing her pretty, imbecilic face against the pane. Laughing, the children swarmed away toward the pillbox in front of my aunt and uncle's building. Built during the Resist-Japan War or the Liberation War—I forget which—the pillbox could accommodate only two or three at a time so the children often fought over who would occupy it and who would scout for the enemy. I took it over easily when I heard the other children leave. I spent a lot of time there daydreaming and thought of it as my home—a miniature universe all my own.

By 1982 when I went to elementary school everything had changed. The river to the east was filled in; the farm fields across the river were bulldozed and turned into a vast construction site. The pillbox was demolished and replaced by a row of smelly prefab barracks for construction workers in filthy clothes. The construction site became the new playground. The children piled sand on each other, collected shiny stones, played hide-and-seek in concrete sewer pipe sections. They ignored several idiots and lunatics in the twenty-four buildings and harassed construction workers' children instead, shouting 'Pig! Pig!'—an English word just learned at school. When their victims stared back in bewilderment they burst out laughing.

Over the next few years, as new buildings sprang up, strangers from the city moved in. 'What an awful place, you can't get anything you want here,' they complained while furnishing new apartments to taste. In the distance more farm fields disappeared and more buildings sprang up. Interesting people arrived. Children from the twenty-four buildings no longer dominated the school. Our new schoolmates' parents came from all walks of life—expropriated farmers turned petty entrepreneurs shared the neighborhood with scholars, scientists, and artists. We children of the twenty-four buildings glimpsed a new world; the sky above looked pale and narrow.

When I was twelve my aunt and uncle swapped their old apartment for a new larger one farther out from the city. By then housing was privatized, the main road in front of the twenty-four buildings was a thoroughfare, and the road behind once lined with peddlers was a busy shopping street. I do not know why I always remember the twenty-four buildings with a gray sky overhead. Pile drivers hammered in the distance. Now and then children's joyful cries burst through the bleakness. The wind dispersed them; the hammering echoed on and on. Under the leaden sky lived a multitude of glib, optimistic, resilient people. Maybe because their life was monotonous they never shut up—on the way to work, on the way home, at work, in public baths, in the farmers' market, in the kitchen, at the dining table, in bed. They gossiped about so-and-so's wife caught having an affair, so-and-so's husband imprisoned for rape, so-and-so's child born retarded because of incest … Irrepressible joy beamed from their faces as they gossiped. It was as if all cruelty and helplessness vanished then and there. Gossiping year in year out about other people's misfortunes, they seemed forever cheerful.

I too was a topic of gossip. From age four or five I overheard talk about how I came into the world. People told different stories. Some said I was abandoned by peasants in the farm fields across the river; others said I was abandoned on the street by an unwed mother; others said my parents abandoned me because I was neither male nor female. When I was out on the street I got inquisitive looks from adults. Children pointed at me behind my back and said, 'Girl-boy! Girl-boy!' One day a stranger waylaid me coming home from school. He jumped off his bicycle—too fast to put up the kickstand—and grabbed me. I heard the bike hit the ground and felt him try to pull my pants down: 'Let's see if you're a boy or a girl!' I screamed, pulled loose, and ran away as fast as I could. Passersby looked on curiously; the creep did not follow me.

I never told my aunt and uncle about it; they never discussed gossip about me. It seemed we were all evading something. I had lived with them from birth. They said my parents were relatives in the countryside far away who had no means to raise a child so my mother came to Shanghai to give birth and left me with them. I asked many times to meet my parents but my aunt always said they were too far away. I asked her why they never came to see me; she said they were too poor to pay travel costs.

Many evenings I sat listening as the wind shook the wooden window frame. That sound calmed me down; I started missing my mother.

The summer I was six my aunt Mira died at twentysomething of encephalitis contracted on a business trip north of Shanghai—they said a mosquito got into her ear. Mira was my aunt's youngest sister. I was curious why she had such a strange name. Later I learned it was a nickname she got because she looked like the heroine of an Albanian movie popular in the 1970s. Everyone agreed Mira was a beauty: fair skin, athletic body, flashing eyes, gentle nose, and hair with a slight natural curl. Maybe my aunt had some Western ancestors: she and her siblings all looked faintly Western—especially Mira.

Aunt Mira always treated me well. Before she took the much better job that got her killed, she made pancakes at a fast-food stand in front of the alley where she lived with my grandmother. Whenever I went to my grandmother's apartment Mira slipped me a pancake and a bowl of wonton soup saying, 'Be careful, it's hot.' Occasionally she came to visit my aunt and uncle, always wearing new clothes with no cooking smell, only light fragrance. When we took a walk between the twenty-four buildings I held her hand proudly so everyone could see us together.

'Call me Mom,' she joked now and then.

So I called her that without hesitation and soon felt she was my real mother though I was not as pretty and lacked her Western look.

After the funeral, when our family held the customary banquet with tofu in a restaurant, my grandmother kept saying, 'I wish I never let her change jobs.' Once the banquet was over and we returned to her home, she ordered her sons, my uncles, to build a fire in the alley out of paper flowers and funeral wreaths to dispel misfortune. It was an early August evening, the sun had just set, it was not yet dark, the breeze was refreshing. My grandmother, aunts, uncles, and cousins all jumped over the fire one by one to purify themselves. She told me to jump over the fire too. I was frightened—how could I jump over such a big fire: Would it burn my feet? Would my skirt catch fire?

'Jump! Jump quickly!' The more she urged the more scared I got.

At last an uncle picked me up and jumped over the fire. I felt my body lifted up and the heat between my legs. My grandmother received me on the other side. Firelight shone on her face, swollen from weeping. Her gaze told me Mira was indeed my mother.

'Mira was my mom, wasn't she?' I asked my aunt when we got home.

'Don't be silly!'

'You're lying, she *was* my mom!'

She said nothing and cried.

Death, just a word to me before, became a fact. Terror stalked me like a shadow. No matter how hard I tried to get away the pretty woman in the black frame on the wall always caught me in her gaze. Closing my eyes, I saw her waxen face before me. Though my aunt seemed heartbroken she showed no horror. I asked why she wasn't afraid. She said, 'Why fear a loved one?' I began hating my mother for rejecting me at birth and revealing who she was only after she died. If like other children I grew up with my mother, would I feel only sadness instead of horror at her death? If not, I wish I never knew her at all. I felt the seed of death in my body start to sprout and grow. At night, whenever I heard mosquitoes buzzing near my ears, I swatted wildly to keep them from getting at my brain to steal my life. I still have this habit though I know mosquitoes cannot transmit encephalitis through the ear.

'Why did my mother give me to you?' I asked my aunt and uncle many times.

'Because you don't have a father.'

'Where is my father?'

'We don't know.'

'Will he come back some day?'

'We don't know, we really don't know.'

For many years I sought my father among the men around me. I thought one day he would appear as suddenly as I learned my dead Aunt Mira was my mother. I awaited the day the mystery would be solved.

Encounter

3

In the first week at my aunt and uncle's I vegetate all day watching television. Programs that should strike me as vulgar trash now seem interesting. My mind is not attuned to television but I watch anyway. I relish immersion in Chinese. Poetry and obscenity are equally pleasant. At mealtime I move to the table. My aunt cooks two meals a day, never repeating the menu. At night when my aunt and uncle retire I chat online with friends far away. After only a week Holland seems so distant as to be another world. My friends tell me the temperature there is fourteen degrees with rain as if winter came early. Their weather report proves I was right to go home. I prefer hot to cold.

When I get home after visiting an old classmate my aunt shouts from the kitchen, 'Guess who I met today.'

'Who?' I guess it was another housewife with nothing better to do than play matchmaker.

'Jianhua.'

'Jianhua? Where did you meet her?'

'Carrefour. She went to visit her father and stopped in to buy food.'

Jianhua is my nanny's daughter, ten years my senior. As a child I wore her hand-me-down clothes. In the 1980s I still looked like a child from the Cultural Revolution—white shirt, dark-blue pants; people said I could have been Jianhua's sister.

'It's hard for Wizard to live alone,' my aunt says, putting

a pan of soup on the stove. 'He changed housekeepers who knows how many times but never found anyone suitable. He complained they were lazy or unreliable and kept looking for one who was honest and diligent, but always failed.'

Wizard is Jianhua's father. Because he was a cricket-fighting expert everyone called him Old Cricket Wizard and, in time, Wizard.

'Old people who live alone are a social problem now,' my uncle says. I did not notice him enter the kitchen. 'Shanghai has a lot of them. In our neighborhood over the last two years the city built three old folks' homes—all expensive with long waiting lists, almost impossible to get into. They said an old folks' daycare center would also be built for working couples' parents who can't take care of themselves.'

Something seems odd so I ask, 'Where's my nanny?'

'Died years ago,' my aunt says.

'Nobody told me.'

My eyes tear—whether at belated bad news or being left out all this time I do not know.

'You'd just gone abroad then and didn't call home much. How could we tell you?'

'What did she die of?'

'Chronic heart disease. Nobody told us either; we only heard it later. It's strange if you think about it. In the past when life was hard she could bear it but once she could enjoy life, she died.'

'Work, work, work—that was her fate,' my uncle says.

'But she lived past sixty, not bad,' my aunt says. 'Back then nobody knew how long she would live. What pressure Wizard felt! He drank every day to drown his pain—old parent, young children, sick wife.'

'Bitter Fate,' she sighs. 'How poor they were. At the end of every month they had to borrow money left and right. We were short too but still lent them money. She was always ill; Wizard is a cripple good for nothing but crickets; and Wizard's mother, living in, was sick as well. Your nanny struggled to raise the children, but her son Jianjun went to reform school. Soon after his release he lost an eye in a street fight and went to jail again and again. Then he got rich from business and bought his parents a villa. Who knows? Wizard didn't move in—cricket fighting and mahjong were easier at the old apartment. Your nanny moved in but died a week later.'

'How does Jianhua look?' I ask.

'Very different. If she hadn't called my name I'd never have recognized her.'

'Different how?'

'Chubbier but looking good—very fashionable, even wearing makeup just to visit her father.'

'Better looking than before?'

'I thought she was prettier back then despite being sickly. Oh yes, I told her you came home.'

'Did she ask after me?'

'Yes, she asked how you're doing.'

'What did you say?'

'I told her you were back, nothing more. You don't want me to gossip, do you?' My aunt flashes an accusatory glance.

'Did she leave a phone number?'

'Yes, she did and said you can drop in anytime but was just being polite.'

My aunt rinses her hands, dries them, walks to the living room, and returns to the kitchen with a business card that she hands me. It feels good—thick and firm with raised characters: JIN ZHILONG, JINSHENG INVESTMENT CONSULTING COMPANY, ASIA PACIFIC DIRECTOR, the card says. I turn it over—it says the same in English—and see a handwritten phone number.

'Whose card is it?'

'Her husband's, of course.'

My uncle takes the card from my hand, puts on his reading glasses, and studies it.

'I never knew Jianhua was so vain,' he says. 'She could write her number on a piece of paper but used her husband's business card, afraid no one knows she married a rich man. Wizard's family never shook the trauma of poverty. Now life is good they can't resist showing off.'

'It's good they got rich,' I say.

'Not just rich—super-rich,' my uncle says. 'I'm not sure about Jianhua but I heard her brother Jianjun's business is big.'

The next day I dial Jianhua's number. Being out of touch so long makes me nervous. No matter how close we were, when I want to reconnect twenty years on with someone time reduced to an image, I need courage.

The phone rings; someone picks up. A shy adolescent female voice says, 'Hello. Who is it you want?'

'I'm trying to reach Yu Jianhua.'

'Who's calling please?'

'Just tell her it's Lan.'

'Mama, telephone!'

After a brief silence comes a laid-back, 'Hello, who is it?'

My heart beats fast. Her voice is the same as her mother's.

'Lan. You ran into my aunt yesterday at Carrefour.'

Another brief silence, then a loud warm, 'Oh, Lan! Your aunt says you came home!'

'Over a week ago.'

'Home is better, right? Much more comfortable.'

'Yes.'

'Drop in anytime you like. I often tell my daughter you were good at school and English.'

'You're too kind. Your daughter must've answered. What's her name? How old is she now?'

'Ting. Seventeen. Next year she takes the university entrance exams. Now all she thinks about is fooling around—she doesn't want to study. You can help me straighten her out.'

I am startled Jianhua's daughter is already a senior in high school. Jianhua as a mother is hard to imagine. To me in memory she is still a teenager.

She compliments me again several times; I feel uncomfortable and steer the conversation back.

'I've been out of touch a long time and just heard my nanny died.'

'You were far away …'

'I want to visit her grave. Can you take me there?'

'Thanks for remembering her,' she says. 'Mom had a hard life.' She chokes up.

When she calms down she says, 'No problem, I'll drive you there.'

'Will Jianjun join us?'

'He may not have time. Every year this season he's so busy we hardly ever see him. There's no telling how long you'll have to wait.'

'He's running a business—of course he's busy.'

‘Business? Just those crickets. In a few days when it cools off a bit I’ll take you to the grave.’

‘OK. What should I bring?’

‘Nothing. She will be pleased that you visit her.’

4

Perhaps because I was born on a day of mourning, my aunt told me I cried a lot as if to lament. The factory had free day care for workers' children but I was not kept there. Day care was spartan and if I cried from neglect I cried all day long, refusing food and drink. When I cried really hard I suffered umbilical hernia—frightening to see, my aunt said. My aunt and uncle asked my disabled cousin to babysit but she refused. So they spent part of their meager salary to hire an illiterate old woman to mind me. One day they got home from work and found her cracking and munching sunflower seeds while I gnawed a crumpled old newspaper. They fired her on the spot. Then their next-door neighbor said she could help. Pale and frail but efficient and sociable, she was not yet forty. I do not know when she developed chronic heart disease and had to stay home on indefinite sick leave. Because of austere social insurance and a family of five her household was the poorest in the building. At the end of the month she often had to borrow money from neighbors. Unable to pay back all the money she helped neighbors wash, sew, cook, and babysit. That woman was my nanny.

My earliest memories are of her—three images to be exact—though I do not know which came first. In one I sit with her in the sun in the backyard: she asks me to close my eyes and say what color I see. I say red. She says it is the color of the sun and blood. In another there are two portraits on the wall—Mao

Zedong and Hua Guofeng: she puts me in bed facing the wall, saying if I don't go to sleep Chairman Mao and Chairman Hua will come to scold me. In the third many people kneel on the ground to watch insects, probably crickets fighting: she holds me and hands me to a young woman with grapes patterned on her blouse. One day years later when I told my aunt this she did not believe me. 'In 1978 when portraits of Mao Zedong and Hua Guofeng hung side by side you were two. How could you remember that?'

I never knew my nanny's name. Everyone called her Wizard's wife. Wizard was a wiry, swarthy, taciturn man in his forties. His penetrating accusatory look always made you feel you did something wrong. He seemed not to like children. He never played with me; his own children were meek before him. Adults were not afraid of him at all, however, and often laughed behind his back. As I think back now he looked pitiful—slightly hunched back, game leg, slinking with his head recessed like a turtle. But he also had rare moments of gaiety—usually after winning a cricket fight and doing some drinking. Then he would tell children of his glory days in the Resist-America Aid-Korea War. He said that when sent to the front he was not much older than his son Jianjun. Too weak to carry a machine gun he was assigned to demolition. An explosive packet discharged by accident and injured his leg. Fortunately the leg was not severed.

Jianjun listened to these stories with great fascination. Hearing dramatic moments described he would exclaim, 'Why wasn't I born in time for that? When will World War III hurry up and happen?' Like many of his age-mates he wished the world was even more violent than it is. They hoped World War III would start tomorrow and steel them.

Jianjun was six or seven years my senior. I cannot remember exactly what he looked like. His image is vague in my mind—neither fat nor thin, neither tall nor short, neither dark nor pale, neither good-looking nor bad-looking. But I clearly remember him getting me to do many bad things—deflate bicycle tires on the street, knock on neighbors' doors and hide, and startle construction workers' kids with paper 'bombs.' We also jumped to the ground from ten steps up and slid down the banister from the fourth floor. More often we went swimming or caught bugs—on sunny days we caught cicadas and butterflies; when rain approached we caught dragonflies and at night fireflies and crickets. We put live cicadas and butterflies on the living room window screen to hear the cicadas sing and see the butterflies dance. We would tie a dragonfly by the tail with a thread and let it buzz through the air around the room. I put fireflies in a washed glass milk bottle, set it next to my bed at night, and fell asleep in the beautiful twinkling of green lights. Sometimes the milk bottle got knocked over and when I opened my eyes in the middle of the night I saw dreamy light spots. Jianjun took charge of all crickets we captured, keeping those he wanted and giving me the rest. I often stared at the crickets in my jar and thought they might have some hidden ability to vanquish other crickets.

When I was out with Jianjun no one dared bully me. Before I went to elementary school I looked like a tomboy—on hot summer days I wore no shirt, only shorts. My aunt and uncle taught me to look plain. To them girlish dress symbolized capitalist decadence. They also raised my crippled cousin this way but when she grew up she made a turnabout. She liked to lock herself in her room, sit in front of the mirror, and put on makeup.

My going topless invited malicious teasing from girls my age. Several would circle around me singing, 'Winter-melon skin, watermelon skin, topless girl—thick skin.' When Jianjun heard the girls say that he would insult them: 'No tits yet only big mouth.' They fled at once. Their shrewish mothers often came by to protest: 'Jianjun must be punished! What he said to my child I'm ashamed to repeat.' Who knows how many beatings Jianjun got from Wizard after all those complaints. Through the fence I often saw Wizard chasing Jianjun with a bamboo broom: 'Don't run! How can this little bastard be my son? You shame us, damn you!' My nanny always rescued her son from his father, who then scolded his wife: 'You're the one who spoiled him! Fuck your mother's …'

Jianjun was restless and talkative, unlike Jianhua. She, two or three years older than he, was quiet and shy. Her features then are also vague to me now. I remember she was pale, thin, and sickly but refined—she liked to tie her hair with a flower-print white handkerchief. To look at her you would never guess she had a low thick voice like her mother from whom she inherited much. The only difference between them was that her mother was outgoing—wherever she was you could hear her magnetic laugh.

In summer Jianhua was healthy as a rule and took me around the neighborhood. I remember us eating frequently—sucking nectar out of flowers, buying dried plums from the corner tobacconist, helping ourselves to snacks at her classmates' homes, and after a swim sharing a bowl of cold noodles with chopped cucumber, peanut sauce, and vinegar she bought from a street vendor. She ate a lot but never got fat. Probably because I ate along with her I was chubby. Growing up in a poor family, Jianhua was vain yet dressed plainly. She had a better-off girlfriend who loved to dress up. Every time we went to that girl's home Jianhua helped herself to lipstick as well as snacks and insisted on making me up too. Afraid of getting caught and punished by her parents, she never forgot to wipe our lipstick off thoroughly before going home. Jianhua was in junior high when I was in kindergarten but never complained I was a burden.

Besides middle-aged parents and adolescent children the Yu household included a shadowy figure—sometimes under the backyard elm tree, sometimes in her bed, but mostly on the toilet. It was the children's grandmother who Jianjun told me suffered constipation, which made her grumpy. One of her eyes was higher than the other and dripped mucous tears. She had a goiter the size of a fist—hence her nickname, Granny Lump. Neighborhood children feared Granny Lump even more than Wizard. I seldom saw her close up but always knew where she was from her shadow and pigeon-like mumble. I did not see the shadow or hear the sound one Chinese New Year's Day when I got back from my grandmother's. They told me Granny Lump died late New Year's Eve.

Remembrance is mysterious. I wonder why those close to me every day for years like Jianjun, Jianhua, and my nanny now have vague faces while those I had little to do with and seldom looked straight in the face like Wizard and Granny Lump are still vivid. I try to make those vague faces clear again but the more I try the more they fade.

5

It is now late August and cooling off. With sunshine every day and little rain some complain it is too dry. I think they have lived with humidity so long their sensibility is distorted. I take a taxi downtown to Jianhua's home, which the driver finds easily.

It is a regular working day. At nine in the morning few people can be seen in this gated community. Several company Buicks roll by. Around me are brand-new thirty-story highrise apartment buildings. In the spaces between them are imitation traditional Chinese gardens with creeks and arch bridges. A signboard directs residents and visitors to the parking lot, café, gym, yoga center, swimming pool, and tennis court. I glance up and see almost all windows are closed, making the buildings look more like offices than homes. In the distance, between two buildings, the World Financial Center looks like a colossal bottle opener. A wind gust between the buildings shakes the trees lining the street and musses my hair.

I press Jianhua's doorbell outside the building. Nobody answers but the front door opens. Stepping in, I see I am watched through surveillance cameras in the hallway and lift. I have no idea who sits behind the monitor watching all who enter or leave.

The door to room 2506 is ajar; I knock. A perfume scent strikes me as a woman in a white skirt and matching blouse appears. Her wavy hair is shoulder-length. Light makeup fails to hide the crow's-feet but her eyes project a womanly charm I never noticed in her before. She is more buxom than I remember. The tight low V-neck white blouse barely covers her breasts and the white skirt is snug around her bottom.

'Come in, Lan.' She leads me by the hand into the living room. 'I hardly recognize you. Why bother with a present?' She takes the box of chocolates from my hand.

'It's nothing. If you don't eat them you can give them away.'

She asks me to sit on the couch; I sink into it.

'You've changed a lot and look completely different now,' she says. 'You were a chubby kid. When you ran your flesh jiggled and bounced. So cute! How did you get so tall and slender?'

'My aunt says I'm too skinny.'

'You've got a good figure. I want to slim down but can't. I get fat just drinking water.'

She leaves the room and returns two minutes later with a cup of tea.

'But the fact is men don't like women too skinny.' She stands in front of the couch and looks me over. 'Now I see you're really not skinny at all. Everywhere a girl needs flesh you've got it. I envy you!'

Scrutiny makes me uneasy. I reach up and take the cup of tea from her hand.

She smiles and says, 'Chrysanthemum and wolfberry tea is good for eyes and skin. You intellectuals who sit behind a computer all day should drink more of it.'

I sip the tea and say, 'You flatter me. Right now I'm unemployed.'

The tea tastes good—light, refreshing, sweet from a dash of honey.

The apartment is high up in the building so the living room is bright. Sunlight beams through the window reflecting countless dust particles. I recall waking up after sleeping in and seeing my aunt hang up washed bedsheets outside the window in dusty sunlight.

'Women over twenty-five have to pamper their body,' Jianhua says languidly from the other end of the couch. 'The main thing is drink plenty of water, get plenty of sleep, and avoid stress. Now I sleep ten hours every night and feel I still don't get enough.' She laughs. Her laughter has the same magnetic charm her mother's had.

'Of course you need a regular facial, manicure, hair-conditioning, and body massage—and can't let up. I've got an excellent masseur who comes here every week. He's booked up but I'm sure I can get him to take you on.'

'Let's discuss it later.'

'You can give him a try and then decide.'

'Wait till I find a job and an apartment and then put him in touch, or else my aunt and uncle will call me spendthrift again.'

'When I ran into your aunt I thought it rude to ask but I guess you're still single.' She assumes the tone of a woman much older: 'Shall I introduce you to someone?'

'I'm in no hurry.'

'You're in no hurry but your aunt and uncle are. I know several rich good-looking men. Do you mind a divorcé?'

'I don't mind anyone in particular but I'm in no hurry. I just want to find a good job and settle down—then think about it.'

'How can a woman live a good life working for others? Work isn't important. What's important is to get a good husband. Once you've got a good husband to support you, you can work as a hobby.'

Noticing I do not react, she continues: 'Actually, the most important thing about a husband is that he treats you well and can support you. Everything else is secondary. Look at me—no stress, pampered body, pampered appearance. It's the best deal, isn't it?'

'It's your good fortune. Not everyone is so lucky.'

She smiles, the corners of her mouth rising high, her eyes squinting.

'What business is your husband doing so well in?'

'Consulting.'

'On what?'

'I'm not really sure. Probably attracting foreign business and channeling foreign investment. He has offices in Shanghai, Tokyo, and New York. He travels a lot.'

Wily hare—three burrows: I suspect infidelity.

'I told him about you: "Sister Lan was very bright and good at school." Shall I ask him to give you a good job?'

'I just got home and am in no hurry to find one.'

'Look at you.' She feigns irritation. 'I try to fix you up with a boyfriend, you say you want to be a career woman. I try to get you a job, you say you're in no hurry.'

I do not know how to answer but say, 'As you like. If it's not too much trouble ...'

'Agreed.' Jianhua swings from irritation to cheer. 'These days he's home. I'll tell him tonight and have him give you a good job.'

'Leaving when?'

'In a week for New York.'

'I mean when do we leave for the Suzhou cemetery?'

‘Right now,’ she smiles. ‘I’m sorry I didn’t prepare anything to serve you.’

‘No matter. I’m already most grateful.’

‘I forgot to tell you: Dad wants to come along too.’

6

She stops her silver BMW sedan at one of the twenty-four now dirty-gray buildings. Seeing fancy cars parked in front of shabby buildings is commonplace in Shanghai: no one is surprised at the contrast.

'Wait in the car,' Jianhua says. 'I'll fetch Dad.'

'I'll come along and tell Mr. Yu hello.'

She says nothing; I follow her inside.

Now, twenty years on, this building, which I went in and out of countless times, seems like a toy house. The dark low hallway ceiling is suffocating. The once-white walls are yellow-brown—splotched with grease and streaked with water stains. Screwed to the walls, handmade wooden mailboxes (apartment numbers and family names handwritten on them in white paint) tilt haphazardly. Bicycles lean against the walls. Next to one bicycle is a plastic bag full of garbage. The cement floor has just been washed. In the damp air the cloying smell of mildew and cooking grease from the walls attacks my sinuses, making my eyes tear.

Like every other Chinese apartment, number 102 has a metal gate outside the door to thwart burglars. The wooden door behind the gate no longer has a red piece of paper pasted on saying: GLORIOUS HOUSEHOLD. As a child I told everyone proudly I knew this family and the man of the house was wounded in the Resist-America Aid-Korea War. In the early 1980s veterans from the Vietnamese front often returned to the factory where my aunt and uncle worked. Their homecoming was more festive than a wedding. Pulled by an open pedicab, the neighborhood committee's welcome wagon with three men aboard—a veteran and two musicians, one beating a drum, the other clashing cymbals—toured the twenty-four buildings. People opened their windows to see which family had a veteran coming home that day. I imagined Wizard being received like that when he returned from Korea in the early 1950s.

The door opens. An old man, dark and gray like the building, stands before me. I cannot imagine he was once a war hero. I remember him as thin but not so small. He is frail and desiccated; an oversize polyester jacket hangs on his shrunken frame. With his hunched posture and recessed neck he is shorter than I am. I see several thin white hairs sprouting from the bald spot on top of his head.

'Dad, this is Lan. Do you remember her—the little girl next door Mom used to babysit?'

He nods and with effort lifts his head to look at me. His gaze is sharp, animating his burnt-out face.

'Come in,' he says. 'Give me a minute; I have to get something.'

'It's OK,' Jianhua says. 'We can wait here.'

He limps inside, turns around, and waves us in.

'Can't we go in?' I ask. 'I haven't been here in twenty years.'

Reluctantly, Jianhua complies.

I do not remember this place at all. Everything is different. It is narrow and dark. Why do I remember a bright, spacious apartment? The living room contains furniture from different periods. Bottles and jars cover the top of a chest of drawers.

The air smells of an old man's body or medicine (I do not know which) and Jianhua's perfume. From the one wall not crowded with furniture my nanny, in a black-framed photo, smiles at me.

Close behind me Jianhua says softly, 'Mom was really good-looking then.'

'When was it taken?'

'When you were little.'

In the next room Wizard is packing something, making a lot of noise.

I circle the living room and walk to the backdoor, open the latch, push open the door, and step outside. In the backyard is a small cinder-block shed. I see a table and a stool inside it. The old elm tree in the corner is still there. It and the backdoor latch are the only things I remember. Along the back wall by the tree is a long row of gray cylindrical one-liter clay pots. The pots suddenly emit cricket chirps that quickly crescendo into a frenzy.

Hearing the sound, Wizard appears.

'Crickets chirping in broad daylight—how strange!' His eyes and mouth open wide.

'So many,' I say. 'All yours?'

'Over a hundred. Cricket season just started. In a few days more will arrive.'

'Don't you remember crickets?' Jianhua asks, stepping into the garden.

'Of course. I used to help Jianjun catch them, put each in a cylinder of rolled-up paper sealed at both ends, take them home, and feed them leftover rice.'

'Rice won't do,' Wizard says.

'What do you feed them?'

'Not rice. Crickets are like people—feed them rice and you make them fat not strong. Bugs are best—dead mosquitoes, flies, spiders.'

'Where do you get them?'

'I don't have many bugs. So I give them bits of boiled pig liver, hard-boiled egg white, raw apple, maize porridge, morning dew. I also feed the best ones bits of boiled crab, shrimp, and fish.'

'Sounds like food for an emperor.'

'Dad, we have to go.'

Wizard ignores Jianhua: 'An ancestor of ours trained crickets at court. My menu for crickets came down from generation to generation. Our family was born for cricket fighting. I started when I was six and though I had no teacher I became a cricket-fighting master around Shanghai. In 1947 when I was twelve I captured a formidable cricket in the Hardoon Garden. You know it?'

I shake my head.

'It's the Sino-Soviet Friendship Building lot.'

'Shanghai Exhibition Center,' Jianhua corrects him.

'It was the biggest private garden in Shanghai; everyone knew it. The owner was a Jewish businessman, a hugely successful foreign adventurer back then. For his Chinese wife he had a renowned Buddhist monk design the garden to look like the one in *Dream of the Red Chamber*. When I was a kid Hardoon was dead, the Japanese had burned the garden, the fence was gone, the place was all rubble—so kids could get in to hunt crickets.'

'What did you do with the cricket you caught?'

'I was elated and ran over a kilometer to the teahouse where a famous cricket assessor held court. His face beamed when he opened the jar. The dark insect stood in the middle, antennae alert, eyes looking upward. He was struck dumb and after a long pause said, "Little Brother, a cricket like this comes once in a century. It's Hardoon's avatar to help us get rich. Let me handle it and every time it wins you get a cut. Deal?"'

'Did you give it to him?'

'Yes, I was still a kid and didn't know the business. Whenever he took the cricket to fight he would let me watch. The first time the cricket fought it was up against the local champion, famous for its quick, deadly bite. The two owners each bet a thousand silver coins. When the two crickets were placed in the fight container ours tore the other one's mandible off. After that it fought six times, winning all six fights. Then nobody bet against it anymore. After every fight the old man gave me ten silver coins. I helped the family make a lot of money that year. My mother and grandmother were delighted and said I was destined to get rich.'

Wizard's eyes glow, his voice loud, his back straight. Jianhua looks fascinated; it seems she never heard this story before.

'I never went in for cricket fighting to gamble or make money,' he says, turning to Jianhua self-righteously. 'When your mother was alive she argued with me a lot about it. I told her a man with no avocation is not a man. Cricket fighting is like music, painting, poetry, or chess—an intellectual obsession.'

'Are you done packing?' Jianhua asks.

He ignores her and leads me to the cinder-block shed. He takes several exquisite pottery jars out from under the table.

'Look at these—they're for taking crickets to fight. The ones in the garden are for them to live in.'

The jars are similar to the others in size and shape but made of baked and polished red clay. Decorated with hand-carved dragons or flowers they have much thinner walls. The lids, encrusted with jade and agate, have handles made of silver or bronze. Many people have touched them—the handles shine.

'These are Ming and Qing antiques Jianjun bought. No idea why they weren't destroyed in the Cultural Revolution.'

He steps out of the shed and fetches a jar from the garden. He removes the lid, gently lifts the cricket out, and puts it in an antique jar.

'This is a real good one, caught locally.' He admires the cricket. 'When this place was still farm fields city people came out here to catch crickets. Our crickets are famous throughout the country. In the old days even the emperor wanted them.'

He slides a small drawer out from under the jar. 'This is for the cricket to drink water from.'

He orders Jianhua to fetch a bucket of water from the kitchen.

'Why?'

'To show Lan how crickets bathe.'

'We're already late. Do it next time.'

'Just five minutes.'

Grudgingly, Jianhua goes to the kitchen, returns with a bucket of water, and sets it down. Wizard gently lays the cricket on the water's surface. Floating, it kicks its hind legs a few times and moves a few centimeters forward, then rests. He swirls the water a little with his finger so the cricket turns round like someone in a swivel chair. After a minute or two he puts a small net in the water, lifts the cricket out, and puts it back in the plain clay jar.

'Crickets like people relax from a bath. After a fight I don't feed them but give them a bath—it's their biggest reward—so next time they fight harder. Crickets aren't like other insects:

they have self-respect but it's fragile. One defeat and they can't fight anymore; some cower, others die from depression. To keep a good cricket going you have to treat it well all the time and let it fight only important fights.'

Wizard talks nonstop as if he never had a chance to say so much.

7

It is just eighty kilometers from Shanghai to Suzhou but our journey takes over two hours. The highway is crammed with cars full of day-trippers. Shanghai seems so big we can never get out of it. Sunlight turns the gray smog a brown shade unique to China. Dust filters the sunlight, making it feel gentle, unlike European sunlight, which strikes the eye directly. But Jianhua complains about the ultraviolet, saying she did not apply enough sunblock this morning and will look older this evening.

'Don't mention crickets when we visit Mom,' she tells Wizard. 'You know how much she hates them.'

'OK,' he says from the backseat, looking out the window like a child obeying an adult command.

'Living alone abroad is tough. You must be strong,' Jianhua says. 'I'm different. I lived in New York with my husband once but never got used to it.'

'Really, when?'

'Five years ago. If our daughter liked high school there we thought to emigrate. But she didn't like it at all. She hated the food and the lifestyle and had no friends. My English is no good; I couldn't even follow television or get directions on the street. After only six months I took her home. My husband had to commute across the Pacific.'

'You must really trust him. Don't you worry he might play around so far from home?'

'When he's here I watch him closely. When he's there I don't worry. White women don't want Asian men anyway. Too small for them. Race can't be helped. White women are big like men and don't think an Asian man's a real man. My husband's plenty big for a Chinese but next to white men he looks puny.'

'The sex industry is big in Japan, isn't it? He does business there too, doesn't he?' I fear I get intrusive.

'In Japan guys get drunk and play around—no big deal.'

I do not know whether she feigns indifference or really means it. I think it rude to press her so I look behind at Wizard. He is still staring out the window lost in thought, totally unlike the cricket buff who lectured me an hour ago.

'Home is much more comfortable,' Jianhua says. 'If you've got money the living standard here is higher than in the West. Shanghai is well developed now. Everywhere you see not only Chinese like you who came back from abroad but also foreigners, everything from vagabonds to CEOs all here for the gold rush. Shanghai is like the 1930s: ten miles of foreign concessions—an adventurer's paradise.'

This tranquil valley between two hills near Suzhou is less than a hundred kilometers from Shanghai, but that paradise for adventurers seems a world away. I never thought I would like a cemetery but I do. The sun shines on white marble tombstones. Some graves are adorned with flowers and offerings. I follow Jianhua and Wizard on the neat stone stairway up the hill; I carry a bouquet of white chrysanthemums I bought from a vendor near the parking lot. Jianhua carries two bouquets of chrysanthemums, one yellow, one white; I don't know why she bought two. On one shoulder Wizard carries a worn backpack. The freight inside clanks with every step.

My nanny's grave is at the top of the hill, overlooking countless white tombstones. Her tombstone is bigger than most and, unlike most, made of fine black marble. Set between two pillars it has a traditional Chinese roof painted gold. An oval black-and-white photo of her kind, gentle face—the same one I saw on Wizard's living-room wall—is printed on porcelain chest-high on the stone. The black backdrop accentuates her bright smile. Jianhua lays the white bouquet at the base of the stone, steps back, brings her hands together as in prayer, and bows three times. I do the same. Wizard takes a box of mooncake out of his backpack, opens it, and places it in front of the two bouquets. He takes out a microwave Tupperware, opens it to reveal boiled young green soybean pods, and sets it down next to the mooncake. Then he takes out a Thermos and cup, pours white soup in the cup, and sets it down next to the soybean pods.

'Today we celebrate Mid-Autumn Festival early,' he says to the photo as if to a living person. 'When you were alive you liked mooncake, boiled soybean pods, and duck soup. I've brought them; eat all you like.'

'Lan is here to visit you,' Jianhua tells the photo. 'She's doing well, back home from abroad. Let her tell you herself.' She pulls me forward.

I visited my mother's grave many times but never spoke to her—my family lacks that tradition. Having no idea what to say, I force words out: 'Auntie, do you remember me? I came here to visit you. I'm sorry I came too late to see you alive.'

I feel a gentle breeze as if she replies. Wizard sits at the base of the tombstone, smoking, again lost in thought. Jianhua lights an incense stick and places it in a holder set low on the tombstone. The breeze stops; the incense smoke rises straight upward.

I circle the stone and see a large engraving of the character 'longevity' on the back. I move away a few steps and notice another tombstone just like my nanny's only smaller, also engraved on the back with the character 'longevity.' I step around to the front and see another oval black-and-white photo printed on porcelain. The face is of a pretty adolescent boy, his eyes precociously determined and melancholy. They seem to stare at me; I feel a chill up my spine.

Beneath the photo it reads: YU JIANGUO, 1964–1976.

Did Wizard and my nanny have another child? Did Jianhua and Jianjun have an older brother?

Jianhua and Wizard join me.

'Who's Jianguo?'

'You don't know?' Jianhua seems surprised.

'Nobody told me. Is he your brother?'

Jianhua hesitates. 'It was long ago,' she says. 'I can't remember much about him.'

'How did he die?' I think I am being rude and rephrase: 'How did he pass away?'

'Accident,' Wizard says.

'What sort of accident?'

Jianhua turns to her father.

'Accident's an accident,' he says, dropping the subject.

Jianhua lays the yellow bouquet at the base of the tombstone and bows three times with her hands together. Except for laying a bouquet I do likewise. On my third bow I see a shiny black cricket at my right foot. I startle; it hops away.

As we drive back to Shanghai at dusk, the boy's face haunts me like a nightmare. His face is my nanny's, his eyes are Wizard's. I feel at home but get the creeps. I seem to hear a boy weeping from the darkening farm fields beside the highway.

Jin

8

I thought Jianhua's promise to have her husband give me a job was idle pleasantry, but she meant it. This morning she calls early to say he will meet me at his office. If the invitation came from anyone else I would beg off. Not wanting to make Jianhua lose face, I accept—I can decline gracefully later if the offer is not good enough.

To say I agree reluctantly to meet him would be a lie because I am curious what this once outspoken, humorous northern man is like now. I attended Jianhua's wedding when I was twelve. He was over ten years older than she, tall and robust. I heard he just returned from study in America and was chief Greater China representative for a multinational company. Everyone said Wizard and my nanny were fortunate to have such a son-in-law and praised the beauty and virtue that let Jianhua marry such an intelligent, successful man. The groom everyone thought so well of had connecting eyebrows and five o'clock shadow. When he came to our table to propose a toast I noticed his extraordinarily large hands and short thick fingers—a physical type rare in Shanghai. Later I heard his race was different—Mongolian. The groom attracted more attention than the bride. Jianhua did not drink: when guests came to toast her he drank on her behalf. Getting tipsy, he told jokes in a booming voice. I forgot the jokes but not the voice, audible throughout the festive din. Even people seated at the farthest tables laughed. That evening I sat in a corner, quietly observing this impressive and intimidating man.

His company's headquarters are downtown in an office building opposite the Ritz Carlton. I take the lift to the top floor—the forty-ninth. The receptionist guides me to the meeting room, invites me to sit down, and fetches me a plastic cup of warm water. While waiting I study the table in front of me. It is bright red and three centimeters thick—two plywood slabs sandwiching a cardboard honeycomb. From two taps I can feel it is even stronger than a wooden one. The company's owner is clearly a pragmatic environmentalist.

Five minutes later a man wearing a dark-blue business jacket, light-pink shirt—open collar, no necktie—and black denims walks in. He is shorter and less robust than I remember and obviously older but vigorous.

'Miss Yang?' He walks up to shake my hand. 'Jin Zhilong. Let's get a coffee outside.'

The lift takes us to the ground floor. We cross the street to the American Center where everything is American—the Ritz Carlton in the middle flanked by office buildings housing American companies, a theater showing American musicals, boutiques selling American fashion, restaurants selling American steaks, a bar selling American cocktails, and customers speaking American English. The supermarket under construction is called American Deli.

'Only Starbucks here. Can't compare with the best European coffee but drinkable.' He gestures me to sit down at a table on the terrace and asks, 'What do you want?'

'Cappuccino.'

'Just a minute.'

He returns carrying two paper cups of coffee and says, 'I'm

sorry, I've got an appointment with a client and can give you only twenty minutes now.'

'No problem,' I say, suppressing annoyance and disappointment. Why are all successful businessmen so arrogant? When they summon you, you have to come and when they dismiss you, you have to go. He probably receives me to save his wife's face and has no intention of giving me a job. I regret stepping into this dilemma. I wish I had thought of a pleasant way to decline Jianhua's offer so I would not have to be here faking a smile.

'Jianhua mentions you often. I'm glad we can meet today.'

He touches his paper cup to mine as if they were wine glasses.

'Actually we met once but you probably forgot.'

'Really?'

'At your wedding long ago.'

'You have a good memory. You must've been very small then.'

'Twelve.'

'I can't tell your age. You look twentysomething.'

'That's flattery. I'm past thirty, born the Year of the Dragon.'

'I'm a Dragon, too, but two cycles older. Let two Dragons toast,' he says, lifting his cup.

This man is good at breezy talk. Since neither of us is serious I will kill a little time.

'Bottoms up!' I say.

After a sip of coffee I continue: 'Of course you forgot me. You had so many guests at the wedding, how could you remember a kid? I paid attention only to Jianhua and you so of course I remember.'

'In fact I forget the wedding party completely. Probably

drank too much. Tell me, how did I behave?'

'Not bad at all. You told a lot of jokes and made people laugh.'

'You mean I was a clown? How can that be good?'

'Aren't wedding parties supposed to make people laugh? Don't the bride and groom by popular demand have to say and do silly things like clowns?'

He laughs out loud, almost spilling his coffee.

I notice I start to speak with a northern accent. Talking with northerners, I speak from the back of my mouth; talking with southerners, I speak from the front.

He notices my accent and asks, 'Where are you from? You don't sound like you're from Shanghai.'

'I was born and grew up here. Don't be prejudiced. We're not all selfish, chintzy, snobbish …'

'Me prejudiced? I married a Shanghai girl.'

'Where are you from?' I think I know the answer but still ask.

'Guess.'

'Your face is flat, your eyes are slanted—typical Mongolian.'

'Good guess. I'm from a small town near Hohhot. Ever been to Inner Mongolia?'

'No.'

'Go there if you get the chance. Eat yogurt, lamb hotpot, and cheese. In case you don't know, Mongolian yogurt comes in a wooden bucket. It's curdled like tofu. Served without sugar it's sour but refreshing.'

'You must be homesick.'

'I left home in my teens and don't care much anymore. I went to Manchuria during the Cultural Revolution, then came to Shanghai to study. I went to New York in 1983 and came back in 1987. In the 1990s I spent a few years in Japan and went to America again. Now I travel between Shanghai, New York, and Tokyo. I often visit Europe as well. Amsterdam's vibrant and relaxing, good place to live.'

'Not many Chinese went abroad in 1983.'

'Few from the mainland. New York was all right. But when I went to the Midwest three years later I was the first mainland student in the university's history. The town had only one Chinese restaurant; I ate there all year and never paid a cent.'

'Sounds like a fairy tale. What did you study?'

'MBA.'

'They had that then?'

'Yes, for a long time, but China only learned about it late. None of my friends understood what I went there for. I explained it to them many times but they never got it. When they heard I paid my own tuition they thought I was a fool and laughed at me.'

'Why the Midwest?'

'Much cheaper than New York. I'd worked in New York for three years so between my savings and a part-time job I got by.'

'Study there must've been hard getting used to.'

'Study was the easy part—not much different from being a Red Guard worker-peasant-soldier student in the Cultural Revolution. Red Guards who went to the countryside to live and work with peasants had a lot of stories to tell. Once they became worker-peasant-soldier students they talked in class and teachers listened. When teachers opened their mouths the students talked back. Seminars in the West are like that.'

Two teenage boys in dungarees covered with cement dust from a nearby construction site walk past our table.

He watches them go by and says, 'When I see migrant laborers I feel akin to them.'

'Are you a born comedian? If you despise them don't be sarcastic about it.'

'No joke,' he replies. 'During the Cultural Revolution I was like them—I left home and wandered from place to place. Call me independent, call me a vagabond—same difference. I respect migrant laborers. Back then we at least had a name: Knowledge Youth, which really meant youth without knowledge. But now they have nothing. Those two kids are about the same age as my daughter but stronger.'

'You mean Ting? She's a nice kid.'

'I don't understand kids today. She's not a good student and can't get into a good university. I told her that if she wants to study in America I can help her. But guess what—she said she would only go if we went with her. I lost my temper and said, "Who's going to study, you or your parents? If you can't be independent, it's a waste to go there. Go to any rubbish school you like in Shanghai."'

'She's still young, no need to force her.'

'Nobody's forcing her. Teens should be curious. When I went to Manchuria as a Red Guard I was only sixteen. I could've stayed in Inner Mongolia but I volunteered to go to the Russian border. What for? Front-line experience. I was ignorant but brave as if the whole world was mine.'

His cell phone rings. He takes it out of his pants pocket and answers in a polite, professional tone of voice.

I check the time on my cell phone. My twenty minutes are almost up and he never mentioned a job. I think what to do next. I don't want to go home yet. Shopping? A movie? Find an old friend to have lunch with?

He signs off.

'Client can't make it. Do you have plans? I can take you to lunch; the reservation's still good.'

I accept without hesitation. Why not? He seems candid.

'We'll eat at the Ritz. There's a Japanese restaurant on the second floor.'

'I thought even the grass around here was American.'

'I didn't know you're anti-American.'

'I'm not. It's just that I was abroad for ten years and am now back home in a foreign concession. It doesn't seem right.'

'We can go to a Chinese restaurant if you prefer.'

'No need, I'm not dogmatic. It's reserved, let's go.' I stand up. 'I still don't know what to call you?'

'As you like.'

'Brother Jin?'

'Elder brother, that's nice.'

The restaurant is elegant and spotless. Japanese are a strange people. They turn mundane things into art—things to eat, drink, or play with become, in their hands, otherworldly. Chinese are the opposite. We make high art mundane as if we understood all along that behind noisy, chaotic, even vulgar appearances lie the real truth and aesthetic of life.

He takes off his shoes and kneels on a cushion at the table.

'Do I have to kneel? Or may I sit on a cushion?' I ask, fearing I can't walk after kneeling through lunch.

'Whatever's most comfortable.'

A waitress in kimono shuffles up smiling like a stewardess. Brother Jin addresses her in Japanese. Her smile shifts from obligatory to spontaneous. They chat for five minutes convivially.

'I'm a regular here.'

The waitress shuffles away. 'I ordered two sushi menus,' he says. 'Hope you don't mind.'

'Not at all. I like sushi. Your Japanese is remarkable.'

'Worse than it used to be. My vocabulary now comes down to ordering food, arguing with people, and flirting with women.'

The waitress reappears with tea and a large flacon of warm sake.

He pours me a cup of sake and says, 'I have to see how much you can drink. Don't tell me you don't drink.'

Still tasting coffee in my mouth, I imagine it mixed with sake in my stomach. Not good.

'Wait a minute,' I say, sipping tea. 'I still taste coffee.'

'A few sips of sake and you won't taste coffee.'

'Don't you have to work this afternoon?'

'Drinking is a very important part of work.'

He pours a cup of sake and taps his cup against mine. I feel compelled to drink.

He drinks his sake in one gulp and says, 'Can't taste coffee now can you?'

'No.'

'How many years did you spend in Holland?'

'Ten.'

'Did you get used to life there?'

'I got so used to it I see only the downside now.'

'If you really got used to it you would see only the upside.'

'It's like marriage—upside first, downside later.'

'You sound like an expert on marriage.'

'Can't think of a better comparison; I wasn't born wise.'

'So what was the downside?'

'It sounds unfair but I was always a foreigner there. It's not my home. It's like a marriage: your partner may be a good person but if together you don't harmonize, marriage is hopeless.'

The waitress brings two plates of sushi with extra wasabi.

He swallows a mouthful of salmon sushi dipped in wasabi and soy sauce. 'Jianhua says you want to work for me.'

'I just want to get acquainted and learn what business your company does.'

'I always tell my people it's not what you do that counts but your passion, ambition, and persistence. When I hire people I don't look at credentials, only personality.'

Nonsense, I think. 'You have to be passionate about something. People are not all passionate about the same thing.'

'People have different passions, of course, but some succeed no matter what they do while others fail. Many successful businesspeople today were fanatic Red Guards.'

'Perhaps you describe yourself; me, I'm a failure.'

'I don't see you that way.'

'I worked eight years for a bank but never enjoyed it.'

'That's because the work environment didn't stimulate your interest—I know the situation in Europe. Work for me and you'll feel different.'

'What do you have in mind?'

'I don't know yet. What would you like to do?'

'Not finance anymore.'

'Finance can be exciting.'

'I'm sick of numbers.'

'What do you really want to do? Let me rephrase: What's your dream?'

No one asked me that since elementary school; I hesitate. 'Years ago in Paris a Gypsy fortune teller said what I dream will never come true. Since then I haven't dared dream anything.'

'You believe that? You must've dreamt something.'

'Age three, popcorn fryer or bus conductor. Age thirteen, traveler. Age twenty-three, artist. Age thirty-three, I don't know.'

'Ever want to be a businesswoman?'

'I'd consider it if desperate.'

'You'll never be desperate.'

I am curious why he has more confidence in me than I do.

'After lunch I'll introduce you to our human resources manager.'

'You never said what you want me to do.'

'After we finish this sake I'll know. Don't worry about money; I'm not a cheapskate.'

9

It is the easiest job interview I ever had. The next day I am project manager at the Jinsheng Investment Consulting Company in charge of Incubator, a brand-new initiative to cultivate startup companies for two years and invest in those that succeed. I have experience in investment management but nothing like this. Brother Jin appoints someone to supervise me. Colleagues call him Little Boss as they call Brother Jin Big Boss. Little Boss handles operations, Big Boss handles money. Little Boss is from Singapore. He is short, chubby, and quiet—the opposite of Big Boss.

The company is small with thirty employees, mostly young and female. I don't like working with women and my bad luck has always been having to work with more women than men.

The first day human resources manager Nancy invites me to lunch. The company is Chinese but Little Boss wants everyone called by a Western name. He says his is Jason and asks me mine; I say I do not have one, which is true. He says make one up. I say just call me Lan. He relents.

Nancy is past forty but well preserved and projects fake warmth, which makes me uneasy. She and I have lunch in the basement cafeteria with several female colleagues. They ask many questions: *Where are you from? When did you go abroad? Why did you come home? Are you married? Do you have a boyfriend? Chinese or foreign? How do you know Big Boss?* When they run out of questions someone changes the subject to buying an apartment; another mentions the stock market tumble; others complain they do not have enough money to buy new clothes. One says a colleague whose name I do not know has it made thanks to a sugar daddy. Nancy scoffs, 'If she has it made, why does she work?' They stare at me and make me swear not to repeat what I heard. I nod but have no idea whom they mean.

The next day Brother Jin invites me to lunch; I accept at once. He says he prefers to avoid the cafeteria—the food is bad.

'Too many mouths,' I say.

'What did you hear?'

'Just trivia and gossip about somebody I don't know.'

'What gossip?'

'Don't worry, nobody's gossiping about you.'

'I don't care if they do.'

'You're above all that?'

'Of course.'

'May I have my own office?'

He hesitates a few seconds. 'I'm afraid I can't grant you that. You saw yourself that we have no spare room.'

'Even a corner will do if I don't have to mingle.'

'Did they offend you or you them?'

'Neither. Too many people talking too much disturb work.'

'Don't take them seriously.'

'I don't take them seriously and I won't tattle.'

'Good you understand.'

'My aunt told me from childhood: "Loose lips sink ships."'

'Your aunt is right. My biggest weakness is I talk too much.'

'People like Little Boss don't talk but observe and remember—they aren't vulnerable.'

'That's just why I use him.'

'He must be loyal.'

'There are ways to keep him loyal.'

He smiles to change the subject. 'I'm often away. When I'm not here you can use my office.'

'Is that legit?'

'Why not? I'll let them know right away.'

The next day Brother Jin flies to New York. I have much to learn and feel stressed. Little Boss plays the martinet and demands a report. Pressured, I use the director's office so I can concentrate. Nobody says anything but I see I just made enemies of most women in the company. They are superficially polite but their eyes betray envy and suspicion.

Fortunately a new friend makes me feel less alien. She is Amy the receptionist. Amy's job is taking phone calls, pouring tea for guests, and booking hotels and flights for Big Boss and Little Boss. I have no idea how we got friendly. Maybe sitting at the reception desk bores her so she chose me to chat with. Or maybe she wants to get closer to Big Boss and hopes to use me. Anything is possible but no matter, I like her. Though her pastimes are the usual shopping and dating she lacks the presumption most girls have. She always talks softly, smiling sweetly. Her biggest dream is to move from the reception desk to the back office but her credentials are weak and she may never make it. So she sits at the reception desk day after day, stealing time to chat with me or phone her boyfriend.

Amy gives me advice on interpersonal office politics and says being on good terms with Nancy is crucial.

'That bitch is a malicious gossip who can make or break you.'

'I know that. She doesn't scare me.'

'You'd better move out of Big Boss's office.'

'I will as soon as I finish this report.'

Easier said than done. A large office is addictive, private space even more. Lately I sit at Brother Jin's big black desk every day, working on a laptop. When the background noise of collegial banter gets to me I close the door. Only Little Boss knocks occasionally and comes in to talk business.

September sunlight is radiant outside the window. I kick off my shoes and sit cross-legged in the swivel chair; the sun's warmth on my body makes me sleepy. The Ritz lion on the roof opposite gleams regally. I wonder what sort of hotel guests are behind all the shaded windows and what they are doing. Working? Sleeping? Reading? Watching television? Using the bathroom? Having sex? Suddenly I feel a strange sensation in my stomach like sake after cappuccino.

I think on my love life the last months. I have had no one. Previously when love approached I felt it coming—self-fulfilling prophecy, perhaps, but I knew. Intimacy, when I imagine it now, does not work: caresses float like dust in the sunlight. I am depressed.

At four this afternoon I excuse myself from the office, saying I do not feel well. On such a warm, bright, almost perfect day there is a fog inside me that will not lift. I decide to walk down Huaihai Road, the biggest shopping street in Shanghai, to dry up my mildewy mood. Commodities, noise, crowds, and empty smiles should help.

Turning the corner onto Huaihai Road I notice an advertisement in the ground-floor window of a tall residential building: APARTMENTS FOR RENT—CENTRAL LOCATION—BARGAIN PRICES—HIGH, MIDDLE, LOW BUDGET. Beneath the ad are two small photos—one of a 1950s four-story tiled-roof building like the one I lived in as a child and, next to it, one of an apartment with a hardwood floor, good sunlight, and a large backyard.

I take out my cell phone and call the agency. The man who answers is an unctuous philistine habituated to sales talk. He tells me how great the apartment is—fully furnished complete with satellite television, perfect for yuppies and expats. Of course he cites a ridiculous price—eight thousand yuan a month—and says I have to hurry: many people are interested.

Having nothing better to do, I agree to meet him in half an hour to view the apartment. It is much closer than I thought; I am there in ten minutes. The old residential compound is freshly painted: the white walls accentuate the red roof tiles. The space between the buildings is wide enough for trees to grow and the breeze carries the sweet smell of osmanthus blossoms. I walk to building number eleven—the same number as the building where I lived as a child. Intuition tells me I shall live here.

The rental agent is ten minutes late. He is near fifty, obviously from Shanghai, with a simian face and bony hands. His right forefinger holds a key ring and (like the middle one) is stained yellow by tobacco; his third finger sports a hefty gold ring; and his little finger has a long nail bending inward.

'Miss Yang? You're early.'

I make no attempt at pleasantry and ask which apartment is available.

'Ground floor, do you mind?'

'Not at all.'

'You must be back from abroad.'

This man is clever. 'Yes,' I say, but regret my honesty. I should have said I am just back from the provinces. That would help me talk down the price.

'Foreigners like the ground floor. But we Chinese think the ground floor is dark, damp, unsafe—the yard is filthy with garbage tossed from upstairs windows.'

I make no comment.

He unlocks the door and opens it. I smell mildew, probably from the June monsoon. The apartment must have been shut the last two months—even the heavy heat of July and August did not dissipate the smell.

'Dark and damp indeed,' I say.

'A room shut two days already smells like mildew. If you open a window and let it breathe it'll be OK.' He opens a window.

'Is it safe?' I see no bars on the windows.

'Safe, yes. I guarantee your safety. A foreign journalist used to live here. Nothing bad ever happened. When he went out he left his laptop behind without closing the windows. Nothing bad ever happened.'

I say nothing; he continues: 'This neighborhood is very safe. There's a classy business district right next to it. They're all white-collar. No louche types. If you're really worried you can have iron bars put on the windows. Won't cost much.'

'Is the landlord responsible for installing them?'

'Let me ask,' he says grudgingly.

Even if he asks I'll have to pay.

He guides me through the apartment—a bedroom, living room, kitchen, bathroom—forty square meters of floor space at most. Its condition is worse than advertised: the floor paint is worn, the yellow walls were painted years ago. The air conditioner, washing machine, fridge, and television are there, all right, but obsolete and dubious. The bathtub porcelain is cracked and chipped, the kitchen sink is made of cement, the stove is caked with ancient grease. The bedroom sports a fluorescent lamp from the 1970s. I pull the switch; it still works. The cold light reminds me of childhood evenings—the family at a square dinner table beneath a fluorescent lamp, quiet and content.

'You don't see this kind of lamp anymore,' I say.

'The lamp doesn't matter. Look at the important things: location, layout, orientation, ventilation. The location is perfect—a quiet spot downtown. Apartments in the new buildings around here cost a hundred thousand yuan per square meter. This one may be old but it has a much nicer layout than most new ones. Its orientation makes it cool in summer and warm in winter. In summer if you open the backdoor you get a natural breeze, very pleasant. And the backyard—even villas in Shanghai nowadays don't have one this big.' He opens the backdoor.

The backyard is the most attractive part, spacious and neat. At the fence are two big trees at least half a century old. The weeds are tall but can be easily removed. In the middle is a small stone patio with a wooden picnic table bleached by rain.

'How do you like it?' he asks with a glow. 'The table was left by the American journalist. Foreigners really know how to enjoy life. Home can be an outdoor café and bar.'

A water droplet falls on my neck. I look up and see several just-washed bedsheets hanging above my head.

'Isn't it nice? People here are all classy.'

'What do they do?'

'I don't really know but most are from Shanghai. Even those from the provinces are white-collar and work nearby. There are a few foreigners as well.'

He seems to want me to believe foreigners live in the neighborhood.

'The location is nice but the apartment is old and needs renovation.'

'Old apartments have human life force,' he says and—knowing his argument is feeble—gets to the point: 'Name your price.'

'Four thousand.'

'Are you kidding? Eight thousand to four thousand—you're pretty bold. Six thousand.'

'Renovate it and I'll pay six thousand.'

'All right, all right, we Chinese prefer doing business with Chinese. I can tell you're well-bred and reliable. You can have it for five thousand. Deal?'

'Forty-five hundred.' I've decided to take it but can't resist trying to bargain the price down further.

'All right, all right—not my lucky day.'

10

I move into the apartment promptly, not bothering with renovation. What made me decide was not the distance to work but the shame of depending on my aunt and uncle any longer. Not having parents I am used to independence. At twelve I went to boarding school and stayed till I was eighteen. Then I went to university in Beijing and, a year after graduation, to Amsterdam. I spent only two of the last twenty years at my aunt and uncle's where I feel like a guest no matter how welcome I am.

Sunday evening I sit on the bed in my new home, feeling lonely. I should be happy but am not. I watch television desultorily and soon turn in, thinking to get up early tomorrow and check out the neighborhood.

Shortly before dawn I have a dream. I cannot remember it exactly. It seems I speak to a young boy; we are having a nice conversation when suddenly I realize he is Wizard's dead son. His clear eyes become hazy and turn sinister. I wake up sweating.

My cell phone says it is ten past four. I get up and turn on the lights. Shining yellow and white from all directions, they do not make the chill go away. The more I fear thinking back on the dream, the more I am possessed by it. I want to talk to somebody and escape the nightmare. I scan the contact list on my cell phone twice but put it down. Who wants a phone call at four in the morning? I never felt so lonely. I could chat with friends in Amsterdam online but I moved in hurriedly and have no connection yet. It is a quarter past ten there; my friends are still awake. What are they doing? Imagining friends far away doing this or that, I calm down. I open the backdoor and step out into the yard. The moonlight on the patio is silver. I call my Dutch ex-boyfriend; the phone rings once. A familiar voice identifies its owner by first name and asks who is calling.

'It's me, Lan.'

He seems surprised and asks, 'What time is it there?'

'Quarter past four in the morning.'

'Shouldn't you be asleep?'

'I just got back from a party,' I lie. 'Drank too much and have a headache—can't sleep.'

It's noisy at his end. The voice is boisterous: 'Your party's over, mine just started. Everywhere in the world, every day, every minute—there's a party. Life's wonderful isn't it?'

'It's too noisy there, I can't hear you.' I hang up; he does not call back. I hear only crickets chirping.

Standing in the moonlight I feel cold. I go into the bedroom, put on a jacket, come out again, and sit on a bench at the picnic table. I look at the sky and wonder whether the crescent moon is waxing or waning. The eastern sky brightens. I go into the kitchen and make a cup of tea. When I return the dawn glows red-orange. My mood brightens. I sit facing east, sipping warm tea and watching the sky. Suddenly the sun pops up between distant skyscrapers. I never knew sunrise in the city could be dramatic.

Monday morning is a new start. I shower, put on casual clothes and trainers, and take a walk. In the park elderly people in groups do stretch exercises. Farmers from the countryside set up produce stalls in the market. Woks in a row of breakfast stands simmer appetizingly. I buy a crispy pancake filled with chopped scallions.

After breakfast street traffic congests. I walk amid growing crowds. The air is not warm yet but I am already sweating. I go home, take another shower, and change clothes. When I arrive at the office it is only ten before eight. I take an empty elevator to the forty-ninth floor, open the office door with my keycard, and step into the director's office. Brother Jin sits at the desk.

Surprised, he looks up and says with a smile, 'Sorry to steal your chair.'

'No problem. Feel free to use it anytime.'

'Why so early today?'

'You're early too.'

'Just back from the States. Still have jet leg, couldn't sleep, came here.'

'I had a nightmare and woke up at four.'

'Dreamt of work no doubt.'

'You know Jianhua had a brother, Jianguo?'

'Jianguo? He was the first of their family I met.'

'I dreamt of him.'

'You couldn't have known him.'

'I visited my nanny's grave and saw Jianguo's by accident. How did you know him?'

'Long story.'

'Wizard said he died in an accident. What kind of accident?'

He thinks a moment and says, 'I'll explain but don't tell the family I told you.'

He gets up, leaves the room, returns with a cup of water, and pulls up a chair for me. We sit face-to-face across the desk. He fiddles with a pen—the one I left behind—and speaks slowly:

'I knew Jianguo through a kid nicknamed Blind—the younger brother of my best Red Guard friend in Manchuria during the Cultural Revolution.'

'Your friend was from Shanghai?'

'Yes, the only one from Shanghai. I was the only one from Inner Mongolia. The rest were mostly from Beijing, a few from Sichuan. I did OK. I got on well enough with everyone. But my friend was different. He was typical Shanghai: light-skinned, neat, soft-spoken—sissy in Shanghai dialect. A guy like that invited trouble. The others harassed, even beat him; I also thought he was bad news at first. But I couldn't stand watching him get bullied so I took his side.'

'You're noble.'

'He was very grateful and gradually talked more. Once I got to know him I saw he wasn't timid at all. He read a lot, had ideas—taught me Chinese.'

'You didn't know Chinese?'

'Before I was sent to the countryside I spoke almost no Chinese. I could understand but not speak, let alone write it.'

'Really? I'd never guess.'

'Seems I'm good at languages. Once the Cultural Revolution started up, you know, school was a joke. Our basic knowledge was poor. Kids from the periphery like me knew even less. That friend from Shanghai taught me to read and write. He used a stick to write Mao's poems in the dirt and trained me to recognize characters.'

'How did you meet Blind?'

'Because I had a good class background—red root, straight seedling—plus ethnic minority status I was recommended to attend university in Shanghai as a worker-peasant-soldier student. That was in the spring of 1972. When my friend learned I would go to Shanghai he asked me to help out his mother and very nearsighted brother.'

'How did Blind know Jianguo?'

'Patience, I'm getting there. When I got to Shanghai I saw their home was in the twenty-four buildings near the university.'

'You mean the Technological Institute?'

'Yes, but I didn't study technology; I was chosen to study English. I still have no idea why they chose someone who didn't even speak proper Chinese to study a foreign language.'

'Your punishment?'

'No doubt.'

He takes a sip of water and continues: 'His mother was good to me. Separated from him, she treated me like her own. They had two boys and one girl in the family. The father died early. The older brother was my friend. The second child was a daughter, sent down to Yunnan during the Cultural Revolution. The third child was only eleven or twelve at the time. He was light-skinned and neat like his brother but small and nearsighted. Everyone, even his family, called him Blind. They blamed his bad eyesight on prenatal malnutrition.'

'I heard children born during the Great Leap Forward famine often had that.'

'Yes. Blind looked like a little kid but was cunning. People all said he was strange, malicious, and sinister. He had no friends and talked only to me now and then. Later I learned he wanted me to teach him to fight.'

'You can fight?'

'Don't I look it?'

'I can't tell.'

'What kid from Mongolia can't fight?'

'Did you teach him?'

'No. He was young but had a stomach full of grievances, always saying he wanted revenge for this or that. I didn't take him seriously. He looked like a wimp. Before his fists were up he'd get knocked down. Nothing I taught him could help.'

'He and Jianguo must have been about the same age.'

'Jianguo was a little younger. Once on the way to his home I caught Blind bullying a smaller kid. That kid looked quiet and gentle; his face was familiar. He must've been some neighbor's son. I walked up and pulled Blind away. He resisted so I dragged him home. When we got there he told me that kid was Jianguo—well known around the neighborhood as a good kid who therefore deserved beating up.'

'Why beat up a good kid?'

'This you won't understand. In those days being good at school was not admired. Handing in blank exam papers was. Blind was vain and wanted to be in. What was in? Tardiness, truancy, abusing teachers, defying parents, and staying out all night were in. Fighting was even more in.'

'Maybe it's the same now.'

'But then it was the norm. Blind couldn't get in with the in crowd so he tagged along with big muscular boys and volunteered to be their messenger to girls they wanted to make time with.'

'Sounds familiar.'

'That's not all. Blind loved cricket fighting and was good at catching crickets. His eyes were bad but his ears were good: he could tell a strong cricket from a weak one just by listening and spot right where it was. But no matter how good he got at cricket fighting he always lost to Jianguo. Nobody understood why. People said Jianguo was righteous and Blind unworthy—

Blind losing to Jianguo was Heaven's verdict. Can't you imagine how Blind must've hated Jianguo?'

'Wasn't cricket fighting banned during the Cultural Revolution?'

'It was banned all right. How could it not be? But banning it is one thing, stopping it is something else. Fans played at it secretly. Having little else for entertainment, they idolized bugs. Gambling money was strictly forbidden so grown-ups bet meals or watermelons and kids bet marbles or picture cards. Material rewards were trivial but spiritual rewards were sublime. Whoever's cricket was champion was treated like a war hero.'

'Did Blind beat Jianguo to death?'

'Good guess but wrong. Blind hated Jianguo and bullied him at will. I knew Blind was bad but I was at university and had little chance to stop him. One day Blind's mother came to the university—she told me Blind joined a street gang and asked me to get him out of it. I asked around the neighborhood and discovered the gang leader was a kid of sixteen or seventeen who boxed with his boys in the backyard behind the building where he lived and took them out to pick fights.'

'What did you do?'

'I had a talk with Blind. He blamed me, saying I didn't intimidate people so he had to find someone else to protect him. I didn't bother to argue; I thought nothing serious could happen. He was just playing follow-the-leader, fooling around.'

I hear footsteps outside the office and see someone walk past the open door.

Brother Jin checks his watch. 'Only twenty past eight. They're early.'

He stands up, shuts the door, sits back in his swivel chair, and continues. 'I told Blind's mother frankly that he would never listen and could only learn the hard way by getting beat up on the street. She was worried and said, "The kid's no good but he's the only child I have left at home to keep me company. If anything bad happens to him my life is over." I told her nothing serious would happen; Blind was just a punk.'

'What happened?'

'What people fear most befalls them. Blind's mother worried about him every day and her premonition came true—only reality was worse than she feared. The university sent me away for a spell in 1976. When I came back I heard something awful had happened.'

'What?'

'Nobody knew why but two gangs had a fight: no street-corner brawl but a pitched battle between hundreds with knifes, hammers, axes, belts—anything that could be used as a weapon. Nobody thought so many could die.'

'Jianguo too?'

'He and Blind both got killed. When I returned to Shanghai early that morning classmates told me about it. We hurried west from the university to the scene and saw bloody corpses. Parents knelt among them, wailing. Blind's mother was running around in circles like a lunatic; I threw her over my shoulder and carried her home.'

'What did they fight about?'

'Trivia provoked violence back then—nothing unusual.'

'How many died?'

'Dozens, I heard. Jianguo's mother's heart trouble started then and no wonder. Her kid was good-looking, sweet-tempered, bright, and devoted. The family always worried Jianjun was trouble and would break an arm or a leg. They never thought their well-behaved older son would get killed. Years later Jianhua told me her mother thought Jianguo feared bigger kids would beat him up and chose a secret hiding place. She waited till summer for him to reappear. Only then was she sure he was dead.'

The sun is already up high. It shines through the wall-to-wall window, illuminating Brother Jin's gray hair and Bordeaux-red sweatshirt. His irises appear light brown, neither Chinese nor Western—I never noticed before.

Footsteps outside the door get noisier. People constantly walk past the director's office. Their banter, giggles, and yawns are the Monday morning soundtrack. Someone knocks on the door. Little Boss walks in. His glance catches mine for a second. He asks Brother Jin if he has time to review a contract. Brother Jin is silent for a moment as if trying hard to pull himself back to the real world here and now.

'Wait for me in your office, I'll join you shortly.'

He sits quietly for a minute, stands up, walks to the door, and opens it. I follow him out.

'Are you free Friday night?' he asks at the door. 'You can join me at a mid-fall party. Don't worry, no bad news. Happy occasion. You'll meet some fun people.'

Soirée

11

I develop a morbid interest in the boy Jianguo and the bloody pitched battle of 1976. Every night in bed the story Brother Jin told haunts me. I guess at why adolescent boys would fight to the death. Each time I guess I see those precociously determined and melancholy eyes staring back into mine. I want to meet Jianguo and hear his side of what happened when he was twelve. But terror grips me like a huge hand. I feel my mind set to disintegrate. I tell myself to sleep but dare not close my eyes, fearing nightmares will seize me. Staring at the ceiling, I think back on childhood adventures with Jianjun.

On a hot summer day two kids—one big, one small—walked single file down a quiet path overgrown with weeds behind an apartment building. The weeds entangled cigarette butts and food scraps; flies buzzed around. We walked about fifty meters and reached a dead end. Suddenly I tripped over something—a large bone! Jianjun spotted one like it. He was sure they were human thighbones. Was there a murder? Were we walking on a graveyard? I felt a chill up my spine and creepy excitement.

We each brought home a bone. I showed the trophy to my uncle. Not bothering to examine it carefully, he said it was a pig thighbone.

I was disappointed: 'How do you know it's a pig thighbone? Look again.'

'Don't I know a pig thighbone when I see one?'

I went next door to my nanny's. She was serving dinner.

'Lan, have you eaten?'

Too preoccupied to reply, I asked Jianjun, 'Where's the bone you found?'

'You think something so filthy is precious?' my nanny said. 'Get rid of it now!'

Our first attempt at adventure failed right then and there. But Jianjun did not give up. On the contrary, he was more determined than ever to discover some shocking secret—a clandestine radio station, a treasure trove, a shortcut to the city. We went to the construction site and looked for sparkling stones containing quartz. Exposed to sunlight all day the stones were too hot to touch. Jianjun gave me a handkerchief to protect my hands as I transferred the shiniest ones he picked up to the schoolbag on his shoulder. He said we could extract diamonds from the stones but where and how, he had no idea. 'Collect them now; later we'll discover how to extract the diamonds.'

One day, finally, we discovered a big secret. A few meters outside the back gate of Guangyuan Middle School was a small trapdoor, well hidden: we never noticed it before. Opening the trapdoor, we saw a ladder. But it was dark down there and we could not see where the ladder went. Jianjun climbed down the ladder but soon climbed back up, saying he had to go get a flashlight. He returned with the flashlight and I followed him down the ladder. It stank of mildew. In the glimmer I saw many doors, clothes hung on clotheslines, things piled up—it looked like a dormitory, nothing secret. We debated whether to continue when an Alsatian chained to the wall lunged at us, barking. We spun around and ran. With that, our third adventure failed too.

After that we had no luck discovering anything thrilling

until just before Jianjun went to reform school. He told me many skulls were dug up at the construction site. I asked him to take me there for a look. When we arrived I saw only stacks of sheet steel glistening in the sunlight—nothing else. Jianjun said, 'Yesterday they were still here. Probably they've been taken away.' Soon stories about human skulls spread among the boys. As to where the skulls came from, they had different ideas. Some said it was a graveyard; others said it was a battlefield; still others said it was a Japanese killing field. No matter what the truth was, Jianjun and I were thrilled. Something awesome had happened where we lived!

12

These days, fortunately, Brother Jin is around to help calm my unquiet mind. When he has time we have lunch together. We often go to the cafeteria on the ground floor of the American Center and chat over sandwiches or hamburgers. He never omits to order cold beer. From him I hear anecdotes about the Cultural Revolution, which was gray-blue in my mind but as he recalls it is full of everyday fun and enjoyment, even tenderness. He asks me several times whether I really I want to hear it all. I say yes; he lights up. He is a born storyteller—once he gets started he looks straight ahead, his voice and mien elated. If I do not interrupt he can talk for an hour or two.

Friday as work ends an email from him pops up on screen: 'Don't forget: I'll pick you up tonight at ten in front of this building. Wear formal evening dress.' I ask what the party is about. He says it is a secret.

At ten Nanjing West Road glitters. I wear a black low-cut evening dress with a woolen shawl over my shoulders. The mild moist night breeze feels warm and cold. Darkness covers the city's blemishes, lending it the ethereal beauty of a reflection on water. How nice it would be if a street musician played jazz right now. Shanghai at night reminds me of jazz—lazy, luxuriant, decadent.

A taxi stops in front of me. Brother Jin lowers the window, gives me a split-second once-over, and opens the door. I sit next to him. He wears a white linen shirt and looks even less formal than he does at the office.

'Where's Jianhua?'

'She's no good at English and doesn't like events like this.'

The night breeze caresses my face. I do not know whether to blame the breeze or what I drank at dinner but I ask bluntly: 'Do you have girlfriends in New York and Tokyo?'

Stunned for a second, he regains composure: 'What do you think?'

'Yes.'

'How can you be so sure?'

'The contented family man probably has girlfriends.'

'Do explain; I don't get it.'

'Men and women are different. Women desperate enough to be promiscuous will have many affairs because men with any experience will spot their weakness right away. But men desperate enough to be promiscuous will have few affairs because women with any sense will find them disgusting. Contented family men are more attractive to women and therefore stray more easily.'

'Where's the logic in that?'

'You know: "The red flag flies at home, multicolored flags flutter outside." You're not home much yet keep your wife appeased. I can't believe there's no intrigue here.'

'You've got a rich imagination.'

'It's not my imagination. European sociologists researched it. They had women vote on which unknown men at a party were most attractive. Men with a wedding ring on turned out to be most popular. The logic was simple: married men don't look desperate—seducing them is a challenge.'

He says nothing.

'You didn't answer my question. Anything wrong?'

He smiles noncommittally.

'My inference is correct?'

'No comment.'

The taxi pulls up before an open wrought-iron gate embossed in floral motif. The five-story French-style building behind the gate looks like it was airlifted from Paris and parachuted into this quiet alley. Brother Jin collects a light-gray jacket from the front seat and asks if I left anything behind. I shake my head.

We walk past the gate and reach the front door. An Asian man wearing black-rimmed glasses and a garish vest stands guard and, in English, asks our names. We tell him. He scans several pages on a tablet he holds up to the light above.

'Your name isn't here,' he says to me in an affected, effeminate, superior tone.

'She's with me,' Brother Jin says, betraying annoyance.

'And who are you to bring a guest?'

'I'm your boss Jade's investment manager.'

The man wiggles and exclaims, 'Oh, Jade's investment manager!' He waves us in.

'Bitch,' Brother Jin says when we are out of earshot.

'Personnel at places like this are always abusive,' I say. 'I went to a chic Paris nightclub once where the doorman was snotty like that.'

As we walk in my eyes light on a willowy young man with flashing dark eyes behind long curled lashes. He has smooth tender café-au-lait skin—a perfect blend of black and white. He wears a semi-transparent cotton tunic with four lappets hanging fore and aft, tight purple pants, and white pointed shoes. Close beside him, one head shorter, stands a bald pink elderly gentleman in a business suit. They are the party's most striking curiosity and every unabsorbed guest takes a look.

'What kind of place is this? Who are these people?'

'We're early. The really important guests aren't here yet.'

He tells me to stay put, slips through the crowd to the bar, and returns with two glasses of red wine.

'This is one of the biggest soirées thrown by the Shanghai party queen this year. It celebrates her new art gallery's grand opening.' He hands me a wine. 'I seldom go to these things but the queen keeps inviting me so I have to show up now and then. Tonight the guests are mostly from the creative community. Didn't you say you wanted to be an artist?'

'That was my dream ten years ago. How did you hook up with the party queen?'

'What do you mean hook up? We met at a friend's party in New York some years ago. She's the only child of a Chinese-American tycoon, has tons of money, wanted to invest in contemporary Chinese art, and asked me to connect her. I know nothing of art but do know the owner of a hot art gallery—I met him in the countryside during the Cultural Revolution—so I put them in touch. Jade—that's her name—fell in love with contemporary Chinese art. Last year she moved to Shanghai and rented the penthouse—a thousand square meters—at the residential hotel on the next avenue. Her place is a warehouse filled with her collection. Probably because she ran out of room she had to open a gallery.'

Several pompous middle-aged white men greet Brother Jin as they walk past.

'I met these guys at Jade's dinner parties. Their job is to fly from country to country in private jets and attend all kinds of social events.'

'Does such a wonderful job exist?'

'Obviously.'

Looking around, I see only rich businessmen, socialites, dandies, and nouveau-riche artists. I feel out of place.

'Let's check out the Russian go-go girls.' I tug Brother Jin by the sleeve to the dance hall.

Strobe lights and artificial fog create a surreal ambiance. Onstage the almost naked bodies of two go-go girls flash and vanish under light beams synchronized with the beat. Behind them macho men in black tights twirl illuminated batons. On the dance floor a dozen young women in stilettos cavort aggressively. I thought *Sex and the City* exaggerated but fact outdoes fiction.

I try to join in but did not drink enough wine and cannot relax. Brother Jin stands aside, watching amusedly.

'OK, let's go,' I shout into his ear.

'What?' he shouts back.

I pull him outside the dance hall where he can hear me: 'Let's go to the garden.'

'Why stop so soon?'

'Too noisy—I need fresh air.'

'Whatever you like.'

The garden is the size of a football field. On one side guests congregate, drinking and chatting; on the other modern art objects sprout—looking at first like dismantled stage props. Between the objects are round dining tables covered with snow-white tablecloths shining brightly.

Brother Jin studies the scene as if looking for someone. With nothing better to do, I also look around. About half even two-thirds of male guests are homosexual. Males outnumber females. Several young women stand off to the side smoking, each alone, scouting with flicks of the eye, exchanging an occasional contemptuous glance.

A frivolous cackle intrudes.

'Ah, you're here! Why didn't you tell me? Too big for your britches!' An Asian woman with dyed red hair and flash clothes, her voice loud and rasping, claps Brother Jin on the back. Must be Jade.

Brother Jin introduces us, saying I am just back from Amsterdam. 'A village compared with Shanghai,' Jade says. 'He's the most formidable man here.' She takes his arm with a laugh like a gong.

Before I can ask her to explain she lifts her eyes toward someone behind me and says, 'Look who's here! You're both from the same place, you must meet!' Dropping Brother Jin's arm, she grabs a large middle-aged lady by the elbow, pulls her to me, and heads off to a group of silver-haired white dignitaries.

The lady shakes hands with Brother Jin and me, identifying herself as the Dutch ambassador's wife. She looks like a housewife abroad with her husband—her children are all grown up so she can enjoy herself at last.

'I love China and have many Chinese friends,' she says in earnest. 'Every time I make new friends I never tell them who my husband is. I want them to like me for who I am, not for my husband's position.' I nod. 'Jade is my personal friend. Not because of my husband.'

A paunchy blond man walks up to Brother Jin—cologne hits me like a wind gust. They chat while the Dutch lady talks nonstop. She mentions her husband in every sentence—husband this, husband that, how bright, how nice, as if she were his PR rep.

'Nice to meet you,' she says finally. 'Please don't forget me, the ambassador's wife.'

I check my cell phone and see the time is half past twelve. Time for me to go. I await a chance to tell Brother Jin but the blond man is garrulous.

A swarthy robust Western woman squeezes through the crowd and comes toward me. I recognize her.

'Lan! What are *you* doing here?' she says in accentless Chinese.

'Ten years, no see,' I reply. 'Your Chinese made a great leap forward.'

'You flatter me. I've no excuse not to speak Chinese now.'

Her name is Linda. Her mother is British-Jewish, her father Indian. Ten years ago, when I worked at a bank in Shanghai as assistant to the general manager, she was a journalist who liked to debrief me. She wanted inside information and to get it often wined and dined me. Our work arrangement became a superficial friendship. She was then twenty-five or twenty-six, rented a house downtown with three other Western girls, and threw all-night parties. Once she suffered a *chagrin d'amour* and went on like a broken record about the Moroccan who devastated her—how this elegant sly guy conquered her with ninety-nine roses, how this sweet-talker performed so well in bed that she betrayed her own blood, and how (it transpired) this 'prince' slept with all three of her housemates.

She looks good.

'How's life?' I ask.

'Work is fine, I'm at a big newspaper now but still single. How about you?'

'Not as good as you. For work I'm shopping around; for love I'm unoccupied.'

'Maybe tonight we'll meet somebody new.'

'Why didn't I think of that?'

'Of course you did!'

'I'm not romantic like you.'

While we laugh a young medium-built Western man in a dark business suit, tie, and glasses joins us. He looks quite serious and also out of place.

'This is Ray, my colleague,' Linda introduces him, shifting to English. 'We're doing an article on Jade—I do art, Ray does investment. They don't need two writers on the article; I'm just tagging along. It was really hard to get invited.' She grins.

'You're still a party animal,' I tell Linda but study Ray. 'You look like you're in finance.'

'I'm just a writer not a banker.'

'Good you're not a banker. I was in banking ten years. Just seeing a banker makes me want to throw up.'

He smiles knowingly. He seems nice.

'Lan does finance too. I wrote many stories with her help,' Linda says. 'You can use her as a source.'

'Nothing to report. If you need a source, ask him.' I point to Brother Jin. 'Jade's investment manager.'

'What are you saying about me?' Brother Jin turns around.

Ray gets interested. Wasting no time, he starts to debrief Brother Jin with professional finesse.

'Tomorrow I'm having people home for dinner,' Linda tells me. 'Join us.'

'What are you going to serve? Bean stew again?'

Linda laughs. She has not changed. Her laugh projects. Ten years ago she explained that when she was young her family ate Indian bean stew her father cooked every Saturday because it makes you fart, and Sunday they never had to go out.

'Can't serve bean stew. We'll barbecue.'

'OK then.'

'Breakfast!' Seeing something in the distance, her eyes light up.

I turn around and watch people move toward the other side of the garden. There the light is bright like a movie set, illuminating round tables on which fresh flowers and lit candles rest. At the far end is a row of buffet tables manned by a dozen chefs wearing white linen hats.

'Breakfast is early,' Brother Jin says, taking everything in. He checks his watch. 'Only one in the morning.'

'Let's check it out, I'm starving,' Linda says.

'Enough?' Brother Jin asks Ray.

'Enough.'

'Let's go.' Brother Jin waves us forward, Linda follows.

I stay put. 'You all go. It's too noisy over there. Here it's just quieting down.'

'I'll come along shortly,' Ray says. 'I don't want to wait in line.'

'Hurry up, I'll hold seats for you,' Linda shouts.

A moment later we are alone. Our side of the garden, crowded a minute ago, is deep and empty. Standing next to a man I just met but do not know, I cannot think what to say.

'You're just back from Amsterdam?'

'Almost two months.'

'Made the adjustment?'

'Barely.'

'When I go back to the US I can't adjust anymore.'

'You're Sinicized by now.'

'I've always worked here with Chinese and lived among them.'

'Your wife's Chinese?'

'No, no, I'm not married. I live in a Chinese area; my neighbors are Chinese.'

'An American journalist lived recently where I'm living now.'

'Oh yeah? Where?'

'Joffre New Village.'

'I lived there.'

'Which building?'

'Eleven.'

'Ground floor?'

'Yes.'

'Then *you're* the American journalist! The picnic table's yours?'

'Yes, I'm thinking to bring it to my new place.'

'No way, it's mine now.'

'Small world.'

No guests remain nearby. Cricket chirps from the bushes roll over us like waves. One cricket chirps loudly near my foot as if caught by the party mood.

'You have many crickets in your new backyard too,' Ray says.

'I know, I like listening to them when I go to sleep. Very soothing.'

'Are you into cricket fighting?'

'When I was a kid long ago—not now.'

'Why not?'

'Since when do I have time for that? Anyway, catching crickets takes skill—it's not so easy.'

'It shouldn't be that difficult. Let me catch one to show you.'

'You did it before?'

'No.'

'Then don't bother trying—you'll never catch one.'

'Shh.' He crouches and listens, lowering his head toward a garden rock. 'It's here,' he whispers, and silently puts an empty wine glass upside down on the grass behind the rock. 'Give me a piece of paper.'

I pick up a discarded invitation and hand it to him. He slips it under the glass and stands up. The glass is empty.

'You're still here.' Brother Jin is back.

'Shh, we're catching a cricket.' I signal him to be quiet.

'Where's the cricket?'

'There was one chirping here just now.' I point at the rock.

Brother Jin holds his breath and concentrates. The cricket is cooperative and chirps again as if to show off.

'Good bug.'

'You can tell?'

'Of course.'

'You can catch it?'

'Can't miss.'

'Then catch it for me.'

'Go get something to eat and see if I've caught it when you're back.'

When Ray and I return a half-hour later Brother Jin sits on the rock holding the rolled-up invitation folded in at both ends.

'For you,' he says.

'You really caught it! I thought you were joking.'

'You said you wanted it, didn't you? It was hard to catch.'

I take the paper cylinder, shake it gently, and hear something scratch around inside it. Unsure whether to keep the cricket or let it go, I place the cylinder carefully in my purse.

'You're ready to leave?' Brother Jin asks.
'I'll stay a bit longer.'
'Have fun you two,' he says, and walks off.

13

Ray and I chat till three. Too tired to continue I say I have to go. He walks with me. I would invite him home but while my mind is excited my body is tired.

'It's not a long walk from here to your place. Such a beautiful night, I'll escort you.'

I acquiesce. He asks if I am cold; I say no but he takes off his jacket and puts it over my shoulders anyway. Then he takes my hand gently but firmly as if in a movie. My stilettos pinch my toes: I regret not taking a taxi but say nothing. Such splendid moonlight makes a letdown unseemly. We both keep quiet, enjoying comfortable silence.

The parasol trees that line the street hide the full moon from view. Moonlight filters through the leaves. Shadowed by trees the Western-style houses of the old French concession sleep soundly. The wind is still. Clothes hang motionless from bamboo poles stuck out from windows. A feral cat jumps between roofs with a shriek. All is quiet again. No part of the city changed less in a century, I think.

We walk thirty or forty minutes—my toes go numb—before Joffre New Village looms in the distance. Seismic dance music gets louder as we approach.

'What kind of ass … are these?' Ray catches himself.

Then I remember the neighboring Red Regime nightclub gave out ads the last two weeks that read: GRAND OPENING 3

OCTOBER—THEME: SPANK ASS! ALL PERVERTS WITH SEXIEST ASSES WELCOME!

'Liberation comes to Shanghai,' Ray says when I explain.

Taxis and police cars wait in a row on the street in front of Red Regime—taxis for customers, police cars for rowdies. On the sidewalk outside several drunk white men sit in puddles of vomit. One stands up and staggers into the street, cursing loudly in Australian English. Two policemen jump from their car, grab him by the arms, force him into the backseat, and screech off.

In my apartment we close all the windows but cannot shut out the din. Ray and I discover Red Regime's latent function. Dance music stimulates animal passion. Exhausted but aroused we skip foreplay and get straight to it, keeping the beat until we collapse. Ray falls asleep. I toss and turn, my mind blank, shaken by the dance music. When I last check my cell phone it is already six-thirty and bright outside.

When I wake up the sun is high. I reach for my cell phone—it says eleven o'clock.

Ray rolls over and mumbles, 'When did the party stop?'

'Six or seven.'

'They're too noisy.' He rolls back over and closes his eyes.

Too little sleep and too much alcohol leave me dizzy and hung-over. My mind wanders back to what happened last night. Everything from Jade's party to Ray's presence is like a dream. Then I remember the cricket in my purse. Is it still alive? I jump off the bed, fetch the purse, take out the paper roll, but feel no movement inside. I panic, open the paper, and see the cricket moving slowly. I sigh with relief.

My bustling wakes Ray up.

'What are you doing?'

'Seeing if my cricket is still alive.'

'You're going to keep it?'

'Why not?'

I take the cricket to the kitchen, put it in a porcelain bowl, give it a few grains of leftover rice I get from the fridge, and moisten the rice with a drop of tap water. I bring the bowl back to the bedroom.

'That's how you feed a cricket?'

'I don't know.' I sit next to Ray and study the cricket. It seems dazed and eats nothing.

'I have to see Wizard.'

'Who?'

'An old guy who knows all about crickets.'

'Right now?'

'Yes. Sleep in, I'll be back in an hour.'

I knock on Wizard's door but get no response. When I turn to leave, a neighbor pops out from next door.

'Wizard is at mahjong.'

'Could you ask him to come out for a minute?'

She goes back inside. Wizard emerges several minutes later.

'You?'

'Sorry to interrupt mahjong. But last night I got a cricket and need to know if it's a good one. If it is you can train it. If not I'll let it go.'

Hearing 'cricket' Wizard forgets mahjong. He opens the door to his apartment, directs me in, and takes the paper cylinder from my hand.

'Where did you get it?' He opens the cylinder and puts the cricket in a clay jar.

'In a garden downtown.'

He studies the cricket for several minutes, saying nothing. His eyes brighten.

'Leave it here. It needs good care and feeding for seven or eight days. Then it can fight, maybe even be champion.'

I know little and care less about crickets, but Wizard piques my interest.

'Thanks so much. Please let me know when it fights so I can watch.'

I leave him my cell phone number and ask him his. He gives me his home number. Entrusting the cricket to him feels like a good deed.

When I get home Ray is weeding the garden. I had no idea the apartment had garden tools. Watching him play the host in my home inspires vague hope. At two in the afternoon we scrounge lunch from the fridge. Then I take a shower and change clothes. He goes home to shower and change and returns two hours later with a backpack full of clothes, shaving equipment, a coffee pot, and beans. Does he plan to move in?

We cohabit the entire weekend. Monday morning we eat breakfast in the backyard. It rained all night long. We cover the picnic table and benches with plastic sheets and sit facing each other. A sudden temperature drop makes one dreamy.

'Are you going home for Christmas?'

He stares blankly as if that is too far ahead to think about.

'I always spend Christmas home with my family.'

'When will you be back?'

'I won't.'

I think I hear him wrong and ask again.

'I'm being transferred to the head office in LA next month.'

My face must show dismay. 'I was going to tell you …'

I want to say something but do not know what.

'We still have a month. A long time … no, a short one. Anyway, what difference does it make? The point is to enjoy it.'

'I have to go to work.' I stand up.

'Sit down,' he says, but does nothing. We leave together.

I arrive at the office with tearful eyes. No one seems to notice. The din of collegial chatter drops me to earth. The day is so hectic I have no time to think back on this morning. I do not see Brother Jin. His office is dark. He probably flew away again somewhere. When I pack my purse to leave at six I see an unanswered call on my cell phone. I do not recognize the number—it must be Ray. I hesitate whether to call back but click the number.

A stranger answers in Shanghai dialect and asks who is calling.

'Yang Lan. Did you call me?'

I expect he dialed a wrong number but hear, 'Oh, Miss Yang!'

'Who's this?'

'I saw Wizard yesterday—you know him, right? He showed me your bug. Great stuff! Look, it's no use to you. Sell it to me, I'll pay a good price.'

'Wizard said to call me?'

'Don't ask too many questions. Want to sell it? You won't be cheated, I promise.'

'What do you think it's worth?' I probe without meaning to sell.

'Make it a lucky number. How about eight hundred?'

Eight hundred! A cricket worth eight hundred? My impulse is to sell but I hesitate. Who is this man? What does he want the cricket for? Resale or gambling? The cricket is worth nothing to me as money but I do not want to give it up.

'Who are you?'

'We know each other.'

'You are ...'

'Yu Jianjun. Remember me?'

'Jianjun? Why didn't you say so?'

'I was afraid you wouldn't sell me the cricket.'

'I wouldn't sell it to a stranger. But if you really want it please take it as a gift.'

'I knew you'd say that. That's why I didn't tell you who I am. I don't want to rob you. Girls don't go in for cricket fighting these days. But you've got a great cricket; there must be a reason. OK, between you and me there's no need to be polite—when the cricket wins you get 10 percent.'

'Take the cricket, no need to talk money.'

'Ten percent's too little? Then make it fifteen.'

'We'll talk money later. Just tell me when the cricket fights so I can watch.'

'OK, it's a deal—15 percent. Of course you'll know when the cricket fights.'

He sounds about to hang up.

'I came home two months ago but had no chance to visit you. When can we meet for lunch or dinner?'

'We'll get a chance. Keep in touch.' He hangs up.

No word from Ray. I know our snap honeymoon is over. After work I have dinner with Amy. She shows photos of herself and her boyfriend taken last weekend and asks when I will get a new lover. I do not mention Ray but answer, 'Everything's fated.' She notices nothing the matter. We talk and laugh as usual.

I get home after ten. A dark figure stands in front of building number eleven. Coming closer, I recognize Ray.

'Come with me to LA.' He grabs my shoulders, staring into

my eyes. His glasses reflect the dim streetlight.

I invite him in.

We sit on the bed. The light is off.

'Come with me to LA. I thought about it all day. I don't want to lose you.'

'Can't you transfer somewhere closer? Hong Kong?'

'It's complicated. They're cutting budget and bringing foreign correspondents home. If I don't go now I'll have to go soon anyway.'

'Wait till you have to.'

'I can't sit on my ass and wait to get fired; I have to be proactive. I got the job I applied for in LA. It's important.'

Selfish bastard, I think.

'Don't you want to live in Beverly Hills? Be neighbors with Brad Pitt?'

I glare at him.

'You're mad at me?'

'No, that's not it.'

'What?' He sounds impatient.

'It took me ten years to come home; I don't want to run off again for ...'

'You can come home whenever you like.'

'It's not the same.'

'Then how can I be with you?'

'Stay here.'

'I want you to go with me.'

'Why should I?'

'I'd like to stay here but I can't. If I stay I'll be a cheap freelancer who needs another job to make ends meet.'

'What about Linda?'

'Same situation.'

'Looks like you have to choose between love and career.'

'You're mean.'

I do not want to argue. I think he is unfair but realize we have been together only three days. Of course the career he invested years in means more.

'I can visit you there,' I say.

'I don't think long-distance love can work.'

'Why not if we want it?'

'Telephone, Internet, airplane can't make up for physical contact.'

'Then what can we do?'

'If that's how it is,' he pauses, 'we have to break up.'

What he says is predictable but gashes my heart. Instinctively I cross my arms on my chest.

Ray is a good American—he believes we control fate. I am a good Chinese—I believe fate controls us. I do not know whether my refusal is resisting or accepting fate. Maybe I defy my feelings, maybe I am a masochist—I really want him to stay.

I give in a little. 'We still have a month or so.'

'I thought you think it's meaningless.'

'It is but I don't want to lose you so fast.'

He hugs me so tight I cannot breathe.

Crickets

14

Another dreamlike week. I cannot stand life without Ray anymore. When he is away I miss him acutely. We love each other as if forever, frequenting little neighborhood restaurants, the English-language magazine shelf in bookstores, the crowded metro, People's Square downtown. We cuddle everywhere. Passersby give us curious, disapproving, envious looks.

We remain oblivious.

Ten days pass before I think of crickets again. Ray is on a business trip to Hong Kong; I spend the night alone. Crickets chirp shrilly in the backyard. I realize no one said when my cricket will fight so I phone Wizard the next morning.

'Didn't Jianjun tell you? Your cricket won its first match.'

'Nobody told me anything. When's the next one?'

'Tonight.'

'What time? Where?'

'You really want to go? Seriously?'

'Absolutely.'

'OK.' He pauses for a few seconds and says, 'Go to the Horizon Hotel at seven. Look for Master Liang—Liang Zengqi—outside the front door. You know the Horizon Hotel?'

'Yes. Aren't you going?'

'I'm old and don't see well. I can train crickets but don't have the energy to watch them fight for hours on end.'

'Too bad you don't see them fight after training them so long.'

‘Training them every day keeps me happy enough. Whether they win is up to Heaven. Don’t worry.’ He senses my concern. ‘Jianjun and I are tight with Master Liang. I’ll let him know—just do as he says.’

‘Is Jianjun coming?’

‘Probably not. He’s too busy and only goes to watch the finals.’

Then Wizard cautions: ‘If anyone asks, even Master Liang, say you’re my granddaughter. Don’t forget.’

‘Why?’

‘Don’t ask too many questions.’

‘OK, I’ll look for Master Liang.’

I am about to hang up when Wizard adds, ‘Remember, when you’re there don’t ask, don’t tell.’

It all sounds suspicious.

After work I eat noodles at a small fast-food restaurant nearby. Finding a taxi takes twenty minutes. Where I have to go is not far but getting there through traffic takes almost an hour. The whole way the driver never stops cursing. Whether he is hungry or needs a toilet I cannot tell.

‘Fuck your mother!’ His voice crescendoes. ‘Die!’

Outside the window a bicyclist glares through his glasses at the driver.

It is already past seven when we reach the Horizon Hotel. A crowd stands outside the front door facing east as if waiting for something. A man in his fifties wearing glasses stands off to one side smoking a cigarette. His eyes dart impatiently left and right.

I approach him cautiously. ‘Master Liang—Liang Zengqi?’

‘You must be Wizard’s granddaughter.’

I nod.

'Why so late? I was worried you'd miss it.'

The more I look at him the more he looks like the bicyclist who glared at the taxi driver.

'Not my fault. Rush-hour traffic jam.'

'Poor bicyclists like me don't have this problem. You truly are Wizard's granddaughter,' he says between puffs on his cigarette. 'You like crickets! Where are the girls these days who like crickets? My students may never see a cricket their whole life long.'

I thought Master Liang was a casual nickname but he says he is a high-school history teacher. When he does not have classes he moonlights. He used to be more ambitious, hoping for big money in the stock and currency markets. But having lost his investments and earnings, he had to sell things like cell phone cases to make ends meet. One day he was seen by a student and felt so ashamed that he switched to 'doing' crickets. I do not know why he calls cricket fighting 'doing' crickets.

'Wizard's latest bug is quite something—could be champion.'

'Which bug?'

'General Guan—the shiny red one Wizard brought to fight last week. You should've seen it—really fierce!'

Guessing he means my cricket I say, 'I came to see General Guan fight.'

'Good timing. General Guan will fight Iron Head from Wuhan tonight. Should be a great match.'

As he speaks a bus pulls up. He steps to the door, turns round, and blocks the swarming crowd. 'Match number three, match number three. Don't get on the wrong bus!' His resonant voice shows he is a teacher. 'Don't hurry, don't worry—there're enough seats for everyone.'

He grabs me by the arm and pulls me to the door. It opens. I am first aboard and take the single seat behind the driver. Inside lights are on, windows closed, curtains drawn. The bus soon fills up with men—middle-aged or older. Master Liang is last to board and sits on a foldout seat by the door.

The man sitting behind me smells like he has not showered for a month. I lift the curtain and try to open the window but Master Liang now standing next to me shouts in my ear, 'Don't you know the rules? Close it now, the bus is about to leave!'

Startled, I close the curtain.

'Before we go,' Master Liang tells the passengers, 'let me repeat our organization rules. Number one, you may not open curtains or windows at any time, even when the bus stops. Number two, you may not get off to pee, buy drinks, or do anything else on the way. Number three, you must now turn off your cell phones and may not turn them on again until the match is over. Number four, while the match is on you may not leave the hall or take pictures. Number five, you may not leave the match early—this bus will collect you outside the hall and take you back to where it picked you up.'

The more I hear the more I worry. I feel like I boarded a pirate ship by mistake. Where is this bus going? What kind of people are these? But it is already too late. The bus moves slowly forward. The stench behind me gets worse. I want to vomit but cannot open the window. Desperation yields an idea: I grab a cosmetic bottle from my purse, smear my hands with skin lotion, and hold my face between them—the scent outdoes the stench. I breathe through my mouth.

Half an hour later the bus picks up speed. Probably we are leaving the city. It seems many men aboard already know each other. They chat amiably about anything and everything—

crickets, making money, political scandal—and tell off-color jokes. Horselaughs and disputations alternate like the banter of adolescent boys after school. Judging by accent, I guess a third of them are from outside Shanghai. The man diagonally behind me next to the stinker talks nonstop about how he caught Iron Head, how it became Wuhan champion, and how he took it from fight to fight before bringing it to Shanghai.

At last the bus stops. Master Liang gets off first; I follow. The moon peeks out behind clouds. Before me is a two-story gray brick building. Passengers get off the bus one by one, still chatting and laughing. The driver parks the bus nearby and joins the crowd. Cigarettes flicker in the darkness. 'What kind of place is this?' someone shouts. I turn round and see dense rows of tombstones in the darkness across the street. I shiver. 'Graveyard is good!' someone says with a laugh. 'Tonight the crickets will absorb chi from the dead and give us a great match to watch!'

My eyes adjust. I see a van with closed and curtained windows parked behind the bus.

'More people coming?' I ask Master Liang.

He affects not to understand.

'The cricket van is here,' someone says.

'Why doesn't every punter bring his own cricket?' I ask Master Liang. 'Wouldn't it be easier?'

'Didn't Wizard tell you anything? Before the semifinals all crickets are sequestered to ensure they get the same food and water and no hormones. That way the match is sure to be fair—like the Olympics.'

Shouting loudly, he orders everyone into the gray brick building. I join the crowd. Once inside we see it houses the cemetery administration. Signs mark offices, conference room, recreation room, cafeteria … Master Liang orders us upstairs into a hall as big as a restaurant with a sign above the door: ALL PURPOSE. Like a restaurant it has a dozen round dining tables. A huge flat-screen television occupies one corner. Strobe lights hang from the ceiling as in a dance hall.

Two men in uniform place identical gray clay jars along one wall. Each jar has two numbered stickers on it. Men converge on the jars, bending down to check the stickers, each looking for his own cricket.

'No hurry, no hurry.' Master Liang speaks into a microphone he holds in one hand. 'Those who don't know their number can ask our attendants.'

'What number is General Guan?' I ask a man in uniform.

'Whose bug?'

'Wizard's.'

'Wizard who?'

I never knew Wizard's real name and feel anxious. 'My grandfather Yu—he knows crickets better than anyone.'

'Must be Boss Yu's family,' the second man in uniform says, walking up.

'Boss Yu has so many bugs. How can we find it?' The first man studies the list of crickets page by page. 'One zero eight, General Guan!'

'I'm right! Where do you know Boss Yu from?' the second man says.

'Yu Jianjun? He's my uncle.' I fear I say too much but they ask nothing more. The first man points to the corner nearest the door and says, 'One zero eight is over there.'

I go as directed, inspect the jar, and see it lifted … by Master Liang.

'Are you its handler?'

'No, I'm an organizer and can't participate.' He looks impatient. 'South-of-Yangtze Number-One Handler will manage your bug.'

A man in his fifties takes the jar from Master Liang. He looks no different from men his age you can see in any rundown neighborhood of downtown Shanghai.

Noisy chaos persists for half an hour. Then the match begins. Master Liang presides. All crickets are assigned by weight to different tables—tables one and two for lightweights, tables three and four for heavyweights. General Guan is on table three, Iron Head on table four. Now I understand the code numbers on the jars—one for identification, the other for weight.

As in boxing most spectators watch the heavyweights. Two middle-aged men sit opposite each other at table three. One meditates, his eyes closed; the other exercises his wrist. The referee, a stopwatch slung from his neck, stands to one side. South-of-Yangtze Number-One Handler is not on stage yet.

At the middle of the table is the fighting arena—a large porcelain plate filled with sand divided by a plastic ruler set on edge. A miniature wall of transparent plastic surrounds the plate. Two crickets, one on each side of the ruler, shuffle restlessly. To me they look almost identical.

One of the two men at the table says, 'Three thousand!'

The referee looks at the other man, who says, 'Also three thousand.'

'Place your bets!' the referee tells the spectators.

'Four thousand on Plum Blossom!' someone shouts.

'Five thousand on Long Legs!'

'Fifty-five hundred on Plum Blossom!'

'Six thousand on Long Legs!'

‘Anyone else?’

No answer.

‘Last call. Anyone else?’

Still no answer.

The betting stops and someone murmurs, ‘Just got started and the bets are high!’

After a half minute of silence the referee says, ‘Ready!’ and takes hold of the plastic ruler with his thumb and forefinger.

I hear nervous breathing.

‘One, two, three!’ The referee lifts the ruler. The crickets at once grind their legs, chirping loudly.

Each man at the table tickles his cricket’s antennae with a hay bristle. The chirping gets more furious and anxious. The crickets approach each other and meet head-to-head. They open their pliers-like mouths and bite each other. One is obviously no match for the other. In less than a minute it turns to hop away. The referee removes it to the jar it came in. The victor stands alone with wings high, chirping proudly.

‘Fuck!’ Agitation wells up around the table.

‘Looks good but it’s useless,’ someone laughs. ‘Some fool bet six grand on it!’

The referee collects money from the losers and hands it to the winners. Soft or crisp paper money moves from pocket to pocket with amazing swiftness.

Another cricket is brought into the arena. The fight goes on a little longer but the new cricket does not last either. Then comes another one. General Guan has still not appeared. I cannot help feeling anxious. Plum Blossom is a terrific contender; it has not lost a fight. Probably because it has not met its match it seems unperturbed.

My cell phone is switched off; I do not know the time. It must be late. But the room is festive and bustling. No one seems to remember being next to a graveyard. More spectators crowd the heavyweight tables. Some stand on chairs to get a better view. Fists shake in the air to the sound of shouts, laughter, and curses. Pressed by the crowd I want to complain but do not know how. Then South-of-Yangtze Number-One Handler appears holding a jar. The crowd quiets down. I hear admiring whispers: 'This is the winner last time at the warehouse!' South-of-Yangtze Number-One Handler sits expressionless at the table, ignoring the whispers.

General Guan's opponent is Plum Blossom. I sweat for my cricket. As soon as the ruler is lifted, Plum Blossom jumps and bites at General Guan. South-of-Yangtze Number-One Handler looks startled for an instant but does not tickle General Guan. In the second I divert my glance General Guan hops clear of Plum Blossom and crouches near the plastic wall, waiting. When Plum Blossom attacks again it jumps away. Spectators hold their breath expecting General Guan to attack. But it makes no such move. Instead it circles and nips Plum Blossom again and again. After five or six minutes Plum Blossom is hurting so much that it dares not attack. General Guan does not pursue but chirps boldly. Spectators praise its novel tactic.

Soon the last match will start. It will pit the victors from tables three and four against each other for tonight's heavyweight championship. The champion will go to this year's Shanghai finals. As expected the match is between Iron Head and General Guan.

'I bet ten thousand,' Iron Head's owner from Wuhan says.

'Twenty thousand,' South-of-Yangtze Number-One Handler replies.

'Thirty thousand.'

'Fifty thousand.'

'Sixty thousand.'

South-of-Yangtze Number-One Handler says nothing. The man from Wuhan looks confident.

'Spectators?' the referee calls.

'I bet thirty thousand on Iron Head.'

'Me too—thirty thousand on Iron Head.'

'General Guan, forty thousand.'

'Iron Head, fifty thousand.'

'General Guan, seventy thousand.'

'Really big match!' someone says. 'Spectators bet more than the handlers.'

Now South-of-Yangtze Number-One Handler gets busy. He twists his wrist this way and that, tickling General Guan's antennae with the straw he holds between thumb and forefinger. The man from Wuhan does the same to Iron Head. The crickets react to an expert tickle as to an enemy challenge.

The ruler is lifted, the two crickets meet, the battle begins. The insects leap forward, seizing each other with forelegs and mandibles.

'One, two, three,' the referee shouts, reading the stopwatch slung from his neck.

The handlers separate the crickets; the referee sets the ruler between them. Once the crickets calm down he shouts, 'Continue!' and lifts the ruler.

Another round, another deadlock. A few more deadlocks and the crickets fight brutally. Iron Head drives General Guan to the wall.

The man from Wuhan radiates anticipatory delight. Then General Guan grabs one of Iron Head's hind legs. Iron Head pulls free but General Guan springs and grabs it by the thorax.

Iron Head kicks and bites hysterically in all directions—and escapes. General Guan again bites its hind leg, holding fast. Iron Head twists and turns desperately; the leg tears off. The bug still fights but the referee removes it.

The man from Wuhan looks at Iron Head ruefully: 'Son of a bitch! That red bug must be drugged!'

'General Guan must've won you hundreds of thousands today, eh?' a kibitzer accosts South-of-Yangtze Number-One Handler, who smiles: 'Not me—Boss Yu.'

'He never shows himself,' someone says. 'What kind of guy is that?'

'Fuck your grandmother! Fuck your ancestors for eight generations!' The man from Wuhan curses louder and louder. 'If he doesn't drug his crickets why doesn't he show up? Son of a bitch!'

Men standing close by restrain him physically. South-of-Yangtze Number-One Handler slips away. The man from Wuhan wrenches free and shouts: 'I'll dig up your ancestors' graves, you son of a whore!'

His voice echoes through the room, following the crowd outside into the night.

15

Back on the bus the man from Wuhan keeps sullen silence. His seething temper deters sociable conversation. I feel overwhelming exhaustion and close my eyes to rest. With the windows closed and curtains drawn the air inside the bus is stifling. As the bus moves along and the ride gets smoother, animated conversation around me subsides. Heavy breathing nearby turns into a snore. I open my eyes—the man across the isle, head leaned back and mouth wide open, looks placid and ugly.

When I get home it is past two in the morning. Not bothering to undress I lie down on the bed and fall asleep. I wake up early and see I forgot the quilt. My head is heavy and my tonsils hurt. I pull the quilt over me and go back to sleep. When I open my eyes again it is nine o'clock. The pain in my tonsils has moved to my temples and my body burns with fever. I call the office to say I am sick and ask Amy to bring me some medicine at lunchtime.

Bored lying down I fetch the morning paper from the mailbox outside the door and return to bed, leaning against the wall to read. I browse the international and national news—nothing exciting. Then I skim the local gossip—nothing exciting either. Suddenly my eyes catch a headline: SHANGHAI POLICE BUST BIG CRICKET-GAMBLING DEN. I read avidly:

The Shanghai Police Public Security Unit raided a cricket-gambling den last night, arrested 50 gamblers, and seized 500,000 yuan. Police sources say it is not the biggest cricket-gambling case in Shanghai this year. They are investigating bigger ones.

I gasp at how reckless I was and feel lucky not to get arrested last night. Good they chose another venue to bust. I wanted to watch General Guan fight in the finals but now dare not risk it.

Amy arrives early with the medicine and a carton of chicken-and-rice porridge from a fast-food restaurant.

'Big Boss lost his temper,' she says.

'How come?'

'He asked where you are. I said you're ill. He said we've got an important client coming this afternoon. Why did you have to get sick today? You've got crucial data in your computer we need for the meeting.'

Now I remember the meeting—the fever burns up my mind. 'Damn, I have to go by the office.'

'Whatever data's important I can get from your computer. What's the password? Which file?'

'What else did he say?'

'Nothing. Why worry? You're so conscientious at work; he should be grateful.'

My head aches. I don't feel up to going anywhere and give her the password and file name.

'I've got to go,' she says after chatting ten minutes more. 'Today is so hectic I've almost got convulsions. The phone won't stop ringing for a minute and Big Boss has a hot temper. If I don't go back now I'll have him for trouble.'

After Amy leaves I force down several more sips of chicken-

and-rice porridge but have no appetite. I put away the carton, get my cell phone, and dial Brother Jin's number.

'Hello,' he says curtly as if busy with something.

'It's me, Lan. I'm sick with fever. I let Amy take the data file from my computer for the meeting this afternoon, OK?'

'And if it's not OK?'

'There's a problem? Little Boss reviewed the data and knows what it all means.'

'We'll discuss that when you're in tomorrow.'

I have no idea what he has in mind. A reprimand, a briefing? I hope I feel better.

'Do you have a minute?' I say before he can hang up. 'I have a question.'

'Go ahead.'

'What's Jianjun's business exactly?'

'Not clear. Shady money.'

Afraid of wasting his time I tell him what I saw at the cricket fight last night in the fewest words I can manage.

Hearing me out he shows no sympathy. On the contrary: 'What were you doing at a cricket fight? Cricket fighting is bad enough, consorting with Wizard and Jianjun is worse.'

'How could I know they're so heavy into gambling?'

'No time now for details but get this: Jianjun runs a gambling den and is a big-time gambler himself. He buys crickets, Wizard trains them, he pockets the winnings. He got caught once. They gave him two years but he did two months—bribed his way out. Getting caught doesn't scare him.'

'That's why he's rich—crickets make him money.'

'Crickets alone can't make him that rich. They're just a hobby. I hear he's got a dog-racing track in the south that's much bigger. My brother-in-law's business is no business of mine.'

'Why not?' I expect no answer.

But I pushed a button. He lectures again: 'Jianhua and Jianjun don't get along—she says crickets are the family curse. Crickets made Jianguo enemies who killed him. Crickets made Jianjun a petty thief, landed him in jail, and cost him an eye. Crickets are all Wizard knows. Crickets upset Jianhua's mother so bad she died. On her deathbed she made her husband and son promise to quit crickets for good. They did but once her eyes closed they started again. Jianhua says she wouldn't mind if they and their crickets were buried alive.'

I knew Jianhua hates crickets but had no idea how much until now. 'I'll be careful.'

'You'd better be.'

'See you tomorrow.'

'Take care.'

I hang up thinking of Jianjun—the one I met on the phone yesterday and the one I knew thirty years ago.

16

Every summer Jianjun took me swimming. Long before we reached the pool we could smell the chlorine. We split up at the locker rooms and met again at the decontamination trough. He said 'meet' secretively as if in code, which gave me a thrill—the main reason I liked being with him.

The pool entrance had a decontamination trough filled knee-high with whitish chemicals. Once out of the locker room we had to wade through the trough to get to the pool. The chemical bath was cold and irritated my nose but I liked the sudden stimulation. Gritting my teeth and squinting, I always saw Jianjun grinning from the other side at the edge of the pool. I was proud of myself—kids my age were brought by parents and some had life preservers but still recoiled from the water.

Jianjun taught me many fun things—how to buoy my body by doubling up in a ball, blow bubbles like a fish, dive to the bottom for coins, and float on my back to look at the sky. Sometimes I saw the sky change color, cover with black clouds, and pour rain. Most people in the pool got out, but Jianjun and I liked feeling raindrops strike us in the water. Outside the pool it was stormy; inside it was warm and cozy with a pleasant smell of grass in the air. Soon the sky would clear and the pool crowd up again. Jianjun seemed to know many people. Often boys would swim to him and say, 'You brought that little brat-girl again,' and Jianjun would have me referee their swim races. Once he raced a guy with tattoos on his back who looked scary. I asked Jianjun who he was. He said it was a guy he just met and not to tell our elders.

One day that summer we played at my home. He read *Journey to the West* aloud but I complained I did not understand its archaic language. Then he proposed to count coins. I retrieved two piggybanks: we emptied the coins out on the floor and stacked them up by size. As we did this he went out into the backyard twice and made hand signals to a teenage boy on the balcony opposite. I thought it strange and asked who the boy was. He said a friend; I thought no more about it.

A week or two later my nanny dropped by our home. She did not humor me as usual but walked straight to my aunt and handed her an envelope. My aunt took it, her expression polite but cold.

'I'm sorry,' my nanny said, obviously embarrassed and ashamed.

My aunt offered a few words of comfort. My nanny left.

'What happened?' I asked.

'You don't know? Go check the piggybanks and see where the money is.'

I checked—both were empty.

'You brought a thief here and didn't know it! How can you be so stupid?'

I cried.

I never thought that would be the last summer I spent with Jianjun. Soon after school started again I heard he got caught with a group of friends stealing underground cables. I also heard he became a thief because of cricket gambling. Then I heard he went to reform school—Wizard insisted nothing else could impose discipline. Now I realize Jianjun did not go wrong overnight. But the news fell like a summer cloudburst on seven-year-old me. I always thought he was a good student at a top high school.

I remembered the day a year before when my nanny knocked at our door. She gave us a box of Big White Rabbit toffee—they had something to celebrate: their son got into a good high school. For a family as frugal as my nanny's to hand out toffee was as if their son got married. The news that Jianjun got into a top high school without benefit of study spread fast through the twenty-four buildings. He was an overnight wonder boy. My aunt nagged me to study hard so I could go to a school like the one Jianjun got into. 'Get into a top high school and you can get into a top university; get into a top university and you can get to the top.' Jianjun's name connoted top.

After Jianjun got out of reform school several years later I caught sight of him in the neighborhood now and then. But maybe because I was older and knew more or because he was embarrassed to talk to me, we averted our eyes and avoided each other. He hung around killing time, looking the typical unemployed youth—flip-flops on his feet, cigarette in the corner of his mouth, hair mussed like a bird's nest. He slunk along, head tilted to one side. Sometimes I saw him on a street corner playing caroms or fighting crickets with other idlers, laughing out loud and talking dirty. He was not the Jianjun I remembered and esteemed who was clever, naughty, and ingenious.

Soon after my aunt's family and I moved out of the twenty-four buildings I heard Jianjun lost an eye fighting over a cricket. I never saw one-eyed Jianjun—he did not show up at Jianhua's wedding that year, perhaps to avoid being seen. Later

I heard bits of news about his arrest, release, rearrest, and rerelease. Those who passed this news along always added, 'What a pity.' I too felt sorry for him but by then I was a good student with a bright future at a top high school and he—a loser—meant nothing to me.

17

The morning after a whole day and night in bed I feel much better. I come to work, put down my purse, and go straight to the director's office. Brother Jin looks sanguine. I ask about yesterday's meeting. He says it went very well: Little Boss will brief me later today. I sigh with relief, wondering if I made a mountain out of a molehill—getting sick is common enough, no need to feel guilty about it.

As I turn to leave he asks, 'Did you see this?'

I approach his desk and see the article Ray and Linda wrote about Jade fills one whole page of an American newspaper and includes a photo of Brother Jin in the bottom left-hand corner.

'You'll be famous now,' I say.

'I don't want to be famous—a tall tree invites high wind. How late did you stay up chatting with that American journalist?'

'We went home about an hour after you did.'

'Together?'

I nod, embarrassed.

'What's his name? I forget.'

'Ray.' I point at the newspaper.

'Oh.' He stands up as if to see off a guest. I move toward the door.

'Say hello for me.'

Two days later Ray returns from Hong Kong.

'How about it? Did you think it through?' he asks walking in.

'Think what through?'

'Coming to LA with me.'

'I don't want to.' When he broaches the topic I cannot help getting upset.

'I'm not forcing you.' He hugs me. 'We still have two weeks. Who knows, maybe you'll change your mind.'

I know I will not but find his persistence touching.

'Do you have time this weekend to help me buy presents for my family and friends?'

'Where do you want to shop?'

'Yuyuan Garden. I want silk and pearls for my mother, an art object for my stepfather. My half-brother says he wants a carry bag with Chairman Mao's picture on it. For friends I'll buy anything special I see.'

Saturday is beautiful. Ray and I thread our way through dense crowds of tourists clogging Yuyuan Garden alleys. Ray, consulting an English magazine, asks where Under Heaven Jewelry is. I laugh—he is more philistine than a provincial tourist: 'That's for nouveau-riche farmers.'

'Let's have a look. The review is not bad at all. Good price–quality!'

I cannot win at being stubborn—let him decide for himself.

We enter the store and take an escalator to the third floor. It is not an ordinary store but a large market with twenty or thirty stalls, each selling almost identical pearls, stones, shells, and handmade jewelry. At every booth sit one or two girls about twenty years old who speak with provincial accents. Each wears a nametag with 'Lisa' or 'Mary' printed on it. The customers are mostly Western tourists past middle age—paunchy men with waist packs and jogging shoes and amiable matrons haggling with Lisa or Mary in slow-motion English.

'Buy what you want quick,' I tell Ray.

'Help me choose.'

Overhearing us, a girl pops out from behind a booth. Her nametag says 'Sara.'

'What do you want? Come take a look.'

Ray glances at me.

'We're just looking,' I tell Sara.

'It's OK if you don't buy.'

You do not know if you do not look—I spend an hour with Sara picking out things not only for Ray's family and friends but also for myself. Were Ray not so bored I might buy even more.

'Am I a good tour guide or what?' he asks as we leave.

'I'd follow you anywhere.'

'LA?'

'No.'

'Just kidding.'

He consults his magazine and wants to visit the wholesale fabric market nearby. Ten minutes later we come to a place like the jewelry store, only several times bigger. The customers are a mix of Chinese retailers and Western tourists.

Just looking makes my head swell.

'If you're buying presents,' I say, 'why not something better and more expensive?'

'Expensive is not always good, cheap is not always bad,' he says like a Chinese housewife. 'If I want to buy something expensive I can buy it in America.'

'Hurry up—whatever you like, I'll help you bargain.'

Seeing a foreigner approach, the booth proprietors are solicitous—some importune to have business suits tailor-made, others to have Tang jackets tailor-made, still others to buy silk items. I brush them off one by one; they glare back. Then my eyes fall on a benign older woman. I ask if she has silk pajamas. She takes out several matched men's and women's sets. They are well made and reasonably priced. Ray wants to buy at once. I ask if she can give a discount if we buy more. She agrees and we buy a stack. Ray did not plan to buy pajamas for his stepfather but finding men's pajamas on sale, he buys them anyway.

Seeing him carry two bulging plastic shopping bags I say, 'Is that it? Should be enough for family and friends in this life and the next. Let's find a taxi and get a drink somewhere.'

'Don't be in such a hurry. We're not done yet.'

'What else do you want? Didn't we just get something for your stepfather?'

'I still have to buy an army bag with Chairman Mao's picture on it, don't forget.'

'All right, all right. Last stop. Take out your magazine. Where can we find it?'

'It's not in the magazine.'

'Then how do you know you can buy it?'

'I don't.'

'So where do we go?'

'You tell me, you've got local knowledge.'

I see an antique market some distance away and suggest we try there.

'Maybe we can find a genuine Cultural Revolution antique.'

'Who says I want an antique?'

'You're really annoying, you know. You don't know where to buy anything but you're fussy.'

Ray follows me through the market full of real and fake antiques. We see nothing related to the Cultural Revolution. I have no high hopes—I just want to get out of here fast so we can take a taxi downtown and maybe find the bag he wants in a little shop there.

'Look!' Ray says. 'What's that?'

At a booth nearby several copies of Mao's Little Red Book stand out. Next to them are Mao buttons pinned to a cotton sheet. On the ground is a box full of Cultural Revolution posters. I approach the proprietor and ask if he has army bags. He shakes his head. I ask where we might find even fakes. He shakes his head again. I get set to leave when Ray starts looking through the poster collection.

'Give me a few minutes.'

He has lived in China for seven years but is still a foreigner through and through. Why does the Cultural Revolution captivate foreigners?

While Ray dreams off into the Cultural Revolution I move on to the next booth—a secondhand bookstall. Up front are self-help books on health; behind them are hobby books on flowers, birds, fish, and insects. Farther on is a stack of yellowed novels. I pick one up and open it: the characters are traditional, arranged from top to bottom and right to left; the illustrations are prints of hand-drawn pictures. It looks like a bestseller before Liberation. I put it down and pick up a manual from the far corner of the display table. The paper is crisp, obviously much older. The characters, printed from prototypes handwritten by brush, refer to things like water and food. The illustrations are numerous and hard to decipher—their style reminds me of the Aunt Ma book on fortune telling by physiognomy.

'What's this?' I ask the bookseller, an elderly gentleman dressed in clean plain clothes.

'Be careful with that—it's antique, don't damage it.'

'What is it?'

'An imperial court cricket manual.'

Did Wizard not say his ancestor trained crickets at court? Studying the book carefully, I understand it better. The illustrations picture crickets from below, above, and the side. The characters explain how to feed and water crickets. I leaf through the book and see instructions on choosing straw used to agitate your cricket, getting it to fight and win, keeping its morale up, nursing it in old age, and letting it die serenely.

'How much?'

He looks at me bewildered, eyebrows arched behind reading glasses.

'I want to give it as a present to my grandfather—he's handled crickets all his life and says our ancestor was a cricket trainer at court.'

The eyebrows revert to normal. 'I wondered why a girl would buy this book. I bet your grandfather will like it—it's a treasure—but I can't let it go for less than a thousand yuan.'

'A thousand?'

'I got it just yesterday and put it out an hour ago to try my luck. Sometimes customers from the cricket market nearby rummage books here. Who'd guess you'd be first?'

'There's a cricket market nearby?'

'Sure. People from all over China buy and sell crickets there. Your grandfather's an expert—he must know it.'

'Tell the truth I really want this book. Instead of selling it to nouveau-riche cricket gamblers, sell it to me for my grandfather who appreciates crickets like nobody else. I can tell you know crickets too and certainly understand. I can't afford a thousand yuan. Can't I have it a bit cheaper?'

He hesitates. 'You can have it for nine hundred.'

'Eight hundred—make it a lucky number.'

'Eight hundred's too low—it cost me that much.'

I know he lies—the small businessman's professional habit. If he got it from a recycling center he probably got it for nothing. But buying the book is not a bargaining game any more. Hassling the old man for a hundred yuan is pointless.

'Eight hundred eighty and we're both happy,' I say.

He agrees at once and wraps the book in brand-new kraft paper.

As I leave the bookstall Ray walks up cradling a roll of propaganda posters also wrapped in kraft.

'How much did you waste?'

'Hundred fifty. You?'

'Eight hundred eighty.'

'Fucking hell!'

The old man seems to understand English and smiles wryly.

Both in a good mood we wander aimlessly through the antique market holding hands in the twilight. We soon reach an exit and see two pickup tricycles parked with Mao, Che, and hammer-and-sickle T-shirts stacked in the carrier. I remember the army bag and pull Ray toward two guys behind the tricycles.

'Do you have those army bags with Chairman Mao's picture printed on them?' I ask.

'Like this?' One guy pulls out a bag from a box on the ground.

Ray is overjoyed and, showing the American penchant for conspicuous waste, buys a dozen bags.

'So many? Who will you give them all to?'

'What I can't give away I'll sell. Thirty yuan apiece here is thirty dollars apiece there.'

'Why not buy all the bags and strike it rich?'

'Great idea.' He flags down a taxi.

Lulu

18

A week later I bring Wizard the book. When I arrive he is carving holes in taros. He sits me down, returns to the table, and continues carving. He concentrates on his work and never asks why I visit.

'So many taros! How can you eat them all?'

'Not to eat, tombs for crickets.'

He picks one up, carves a hole in its top with a kitchen knife, and twists the knife to make the hole wider and deeper. Satisfied, he puts it in a basket on the floor and picks up another. I pull up a chair and help him.

'In late October crickets get old,' he says. 'Letting them die in taro tombs keeps them warm and safe from starvation.'

I ask if General Guan won the finals.

'Yes,' he says without emotion as if the win was expected.

He picks up a large, full-bodied taro, lifts it high, and studies it against the light. 'Let's give General Guan this one.'

He spends twice the usual time carving and puts it in the center of the basket. It is larger than the others and seems lonely. Looking into the carved hole, I see a mysterious white-purple color.

Once the basket is full of carved taros I say, 'I have something for you,' and hand him the book.

He wipes both hands on his smock, takes the book from my hand, carefully removes the wrapping, and gently leafs through the crisp yellow pages. I expect him to light up but see tears in his eyes.

'Where did you get this?'

'From a secondhand bookseller near Yuyuan Garden.'

He drifts off in thought and covers his face with both hands; his shoulders shudder. When the sobbing stops he gets up and walks to the bathroom. He returns a few minutes later, tears wiped dry and hands washed clean.

He picks the book up and says, 'This is the cricket book bequeathed by my ancestors and confiscated during the Cultural Revolution.'

'I sensed a connection with you when I bought it.'

'Who's the bookseller?'

'An old man about seventy, wears glasses, looks intellectual.'

He thinks a moment and shakes his head.

'Are you sure it's the book you lost?'

'Yes. I thought it was burned long ago. It's a miracle it survived.'

'Why didn't the Red Guards burn it?'

'Not Red Guards, kids making trouble.'

'I can go back and ask where it came from. The bookseller seems nice.'

'No need, just curious.'

He stares at the book, fondling it gently as if wishing not to leave a fingerprint. The grandfather clock ticking accentuates the stillness. I get up to leave. He looks at me and smiles; his eyes fall back on the book. At the door I hear: 'Thank you!'

'My pleasure,' I say, closing the door.

That evening when Ray gets home I tell him about the cricket book.

'Let's ask the bookseller,' he suggests.

Thinking Wizard must want to know how the book got there, I agree.

Saturday we visit the bookseller. I have no sense of direction; fortunately Ray remembers the way. Again I follow this foreign tour guide; we find the stall easily.

The old man remembers and asks, 'Did your grandfather like the present?'

'Very much,' I say, trying to recall my cover story. 'He asked me to ask where you got it.'

'Where I got it? From a secondhand bookstore, where else?'

'Which one?'

'If your grandfather wants to browse cricket books there he's wasting his time. I'm tight with the owner who knows what books I want. If your grandfather wants more cricket books send him to me—I have them all. Antique or modern, they won't be too expensive.'

'It's not that. My grandfather's cricket mastery is in his head. He needs no books. He just wants to know how this one survived the Cultural Revolution.'

'That I don't know. Some books were lost then, some were kept secretly—nothing unusual.'

'What store did you get it from?'

'On Jiangxi Middle Road, corner of Guangdong Road, near the Bund.'

'What's it called?'

'Don't remember. I go there every week but never noticed the name. The man behind the counter is the owner—Mr. Wang, about my age. Just say Old Qu sent you.'

'Many thanks. We'll go there right now.'

I have been to the Bund countless times but paid no attention to the winding, narrow, old streets with tram wires overhead behind the massive colonial buildings. The street we are on is like the mouth of an old man who never brushes his teeth—black, yellow, filthy, putrid. Dilapidated houses are like snaggleteeth. It is congested—car horns and bike bells are cacophonous. A stench wafts through the open taxi window. No idea who urinated, defecated, or discarded rotten shrimp. I cannot imagine a quality secondhand bookstore here.

Guangdong Road is a hundred meters ahead but the taxi driver lets us out, saying we can get there faster on foot. Some fashionable people, Chinese and foreign, pass by. We follow them until they pull off into a doorway with a billboard out front announcing a new exhibition at Jade's art gallery. We see Guangdong Road but no sign of a secondhand bookstore. The houses opposite look residential—clothes hang outside the windows.

'Did the old man remember it wrong?'

'Let's ask,' Ray says.

I walk into Jade's gallery and ask a man at the reception desk. He has no idea what I am talking about. Outside the gallery I ask several passersby. Still no one knows.

'Seems we can't find it.'

'Don't be so impatient.' Ray's professional attitude forbids surrender. 'Let's cross the street and ask people who live here.'

We dodge heavy traffic and arrive beneath a wooden window frame with pajamas hanging in front. A woman leans out to collect them. I ask her where the secondhand bookstore is. She points downstairs. There is indeed a small door with a sign that says: NANLING BOOK COMPANY. As we step in a mildew smell assails us. Between stacks of yellowed books is a small nearsighted man.

'You must be Mr. Wang.' I walk up. 'Old Qu sent me.'

He smiles. 'What book are you looking for?'

'I'm not looking for a book. I just want to know where a book you sold Old Qu came from.'

'Which one?'

'A Qing cricket book.'

'When did he buy it from me?'

'We bought it from Old Qu last Saturday. He said he got it from you the day before—23 October.'

He opens his account book, moves a ruler down the page, and stops.

'The 23rd—yes I sold Old Qu that book.'

Ray squeezes my hand. Ordinarily when he hears standard Mandarin he misses half. But today he seems to understand the bookseller's Shanghai Mandarin.

'Where did you get it?'

'Why do you want to know?'

'My grandfather says our family lost it in the Cultural Revolution—he wants to know how it survived.'

'Let me check for you.' He consults his account book again. 'On 17 October a Mr. Yang sold it to me. He brought in many other books as well.' He lifts several novels from the floor near his feet. 'Check whether anything else here belonged to your family.'

I lay the books out on his worktable. All are translations: *Pushkin Collected Poems*, *Les Misérables*, *Jean-Christophe*, *Le Père Goriot*, *Eugénie Grandet*, *Hard Times* ... As I check them over he brings in a stack of old magazines. I put down the book in my hand and look through them: *Story Time*, *Popular Movies*, *Foreign Art* ... Among them is the Cultural Revolution children's cartoon booklet *Hai Hong*. I show it to Ray, asking if he knows what a Little Red Guard is.

‘That effervescent little girl on the cover with big eyes and pigtails,’ he says, opening the booklet and scanning it amusedly.

The cartoons are all too familiar to me. I take the booklet back and check the front endpaper but find nothing. Then I take *Pushkin Collected Poems* and, on the front endpaper, find my crippled cousin’s signature.

I had no idea my family sequestered the cricket book. Did my cousin hide it? She never touched a cricket. Did my uncle hide it? I never saw him handle crickets. My aunt is even less likely. How did my family get hold of it?

‘Are you sure Mr. Yang brought the cricket book here with the others?’

‘No doubt about it, I remember clearly. He had almost nothing of value; only the cricket book was worth money. I gave him fifty yuan. He looked like he won first prize in the lottery.’

‘Mr. Yang is seventysomething, bald, wears glasses, has a round face?’

‘Exactly.’

19

The next afternoon, Sunday, I drop by my aunt and uncle's. He is at the dining table reading a newspaper. She is on the couch absorbed in television while absent-mindedly peeling boiled chestnuts from a bowl on the coffee table in front of her.

'You're here,' she says, eyes glued to the screen.

I glance and see a costume soap opera, walk to the dining table, take a section of the newspaper, and sit down. After ten or fifteen minutes I hear the end theme song of the soap, get up, and sit next to my aunt.

'I want to ask you something.'

She turns off the television and looks at me: 'I'm well past seventy, I expect nothing more from life: I just want to see you married before I'm buried.'

'I'm not here to discuss that.'

Her eyes flash bitterness as if I stole her last hope.

'What is it you want to ask?'

'Did my uncle sell a batch of old books two weeks ago?'

'Yes, we cleaned your cousin's room. She had a lot of books. No point keeping them.'

'Did you see the cricket book?'

Her eyes flare and cool. 'Ask your uncle, I don't know.'

He gives her an accusatory look and approaches with deliberate slowness. 'What did you say?'

I repeat my question.

'I can't remember—I sold so many books.'

'Really don't remember? The bookseller said he gave you fifty yuan.'

'The bookseller? How do you know him?'

I recount how I found the cricket book.

'It's Wizard's?'

'Yes.'

'Wizard?' My aunt gives my uncle a nervous glance.

'Can't be.' His voice tails off. 'How's it possible?'

'Anything wrong?'

'Nothing,' they say in chorus.

'Wizard kept a "poisonous weed" in the house—asking to get killed,' she adds uneasily.

'How did my cousin get it?'

'Who knows?' she says.

'Your cousin is gone.' He lowers his eyes. 'No one left we can ask.'

'No idea?'

'No.'

'Maybe someone in Wizard's family left the book here.'

'Maybe.'

'Not likely,' I say on second thought. 'They love crickets so much and would be devastated to lose it.'

'Right.'

'He said kids stole it. My cousin's classmates?'

'Maybe.'

'Does it make any difference?' my aunt cuts in.

'Don't you find the theft suspicious?'

'Lots of things were confiscated during the Cultural Revolution.'

'I doubt it was confiscated.'

'You think we stole it?'

I want to ask more but she interrupts: 'Let it rest.'

Their evasion alerts me. Something to hide? I recall the same evasive tone when as a child I asked about my father. Does the cricket book have something to do with him?

When I get home Ray is waiting to go out. We go to a neighborhood restaurant for dinner and, as usual, order diced chicken with peanuts and eggplant sautéed with spicy garlic sauce—his favorite.

The owner returns with two plates. 'Your food is ready, handsome.' She winks at Ray. He smiles shyly.

'You two make a good match—so neat and intellectual,' she says, setting the plates on the table. 'Enjoy, handsome!'

'She's nice,' Ray says. 'We should've ordered more.'

'Look at you.' I shake my head. 'Flattery makes you giddy.'

My cell phone rings; I pick up.

'Drop by when convenient,' Wizard says. 'I have something important for you.'

'I'll be there next week some day after work.'

'No hurry, anytime.' He hangs up.

'Who's that?'

'Wizard.'

'Cricket book?'

'Probably.'

The next afternoon I go out with Little Boss to see a client. Business concludes early. He says he has something that needs taking care of and wants to leave. I am in no mood to go back to the office either and get a taxi to Wizard's.

The driver stops short of the twenty-four buildings, saying he cannot drive closer because of construction work on the sewer pipes. I pay up and get out. It starts to rain. I have no umbrella with me. The rain is not heavy, fortunately, but dense, tickling my face uncomfortably. The ground is all mud drifts and puddles. I tiptoe past the construction site toward Wizard's building.

'I'll meet you tonight by the river,' a familiar voice calls from the corner ground-floor apartment.

'Drowned man's ghost is coming!' a gleeful children's cry answers through the gentle curtain of rain.

School is out. Children's cries everywhere sound the same. Loony Lulu must have stood at the window talking to herself for thirty years. She would be about fifty now. I cannot imagine what she looks like. In my mind's eye she is still a girl of twentysomething, beautiful and forlorn. Time seems to have stopped. She repeats what she used to say long ago and I remember her as she looked when I was a child.

When Wizard invites me in I see the cricket book lying open on a sheet of kraft paper atop the living room table.

'So happy this book found its owner,' I say.

He smiles, walks to a chest of drawers, opens it, takes out a large manila envelope, and hands it to me.

'What's this?'

'From Jianjun.'

I open it and count fifteen thick stacks of hundred yuan bills, each stack bound with a rubber band. On the envelope it says 'One hundred fifty thousand yuan.'

'Why all this money?'

'General Guan won it for you.'

'What?'

'Jianjun said it's your finder's fee.'

'I thought he was joking.'

'A 15-percent cut for supplying a winning cricket is the going rate in this business.'

'I can't accept it.'

'Take it. There's no point leaving it here. Jianjun won't take it back.'

'How can I accept so much money?'

'Take it or Jianjun will blame me.'

'No I can't.'

'Take it, take it.'

Wizard insists I take the money no matter how hard I try to refuse. I am tempted—pocketing a hundred and fifty thousand tax-free feels good. But I am ambivalent about making more than half a year's hard-earned salary off a little bug I got as a present. At last, unable to confute Wizard's argument or suppress my own greed, I accept the money.

Maybe wanting to reciprocate, I confess to Wizard: 'I visited the bookseller.'

'Oh?'

'It was my uncle who sold him the cricket book.'

'Your uncle?' His eyes narrow.

'I asked him about it yesterday.'

'What did he say?'

'He said he found it in my cousin's room—no idea how it got there.'

'All those years the stolen book was right next door.' He sighs.

'How was it stolen exactly?'

'I don't quite know.' He looks down, trying to recall. 'One day I was at work. My son rushed into the factory to tell me something bad was happening at home. I rode straight back on my bicycle but got there too late: the book was snatched by a gang of kids. Strange, we never told anyone we had that book in the house. How could they know?'

'Do you know who those kids were?'

'You wouldn't know them if I told you.'

'Was Jianguo the son who told you?'

'Jianguo?'

'Brother Jin mentioned him.'

'Where did my son-in-law get such a big mouth?'

I realize I say too much and shut up. But I am almost certain the theft had to do with Jianguo and Blind.

'What year did it happen?'

'1975—near the end of the Cultural Revolution. When the Cultural Revolution was over we thought the book would turn up unless someone destroyed it. Back then many confiscated things returned to their owners—but not the book. We thought it was burned.'

I recall Brother Jin saying Jianguo and Blind both perished in the spring of 1976. The book was stolen in 1975. Might these two facts be connected?

'What happened next?'

'I don't remember.'

'Didn't you look for it?'

'What? Look for a "poisonous weed"—who'd dare? A mute can't speak bitterness.'

Wizard obviously does not want to discuss it. 'Let it rest, let it rest,' he repeats. 'Good the book is back. Don't take the past too seriously.'

I rephrase, trying to be indirect; but he keeps silent. I fear he will say nothing if I press him and after several minutes get up to leave, thinking I can better ask Brother Jin the next time I see him: he may have some clues.

It rains harder. I cover my head with one hand and clutch my hundred fifty thousand yuan purse in the other, tiptoeing through the rain again in high heels. My pant legs get wet and splattered with mud. When I reach Loony Lulu's building she is still behind the window saying, 'I'll meet you tonight by the river.' The rain almost drowns out her voice. No one is on the street. Children are indoors, adults are at work.

I stand in the entrance of her apartment building, catching my breath while taking shelter. Impulsively I try to see what she looks like at fifty. Leaning sideways, I peek through the open window. Behind black iron bars is a fat face swollen like a steamed bun. The features are normal but crowded together in the middle. Dull empty eyes look straight ahead not seeing me at all. When the mouth opens to speak it reveals a few remaining teeth. The hair is greasy and stringy, exposing white scalp—strangely there is not a single white hair. She wears an unseasonable wadded cotton jacket; the dandruff on her shoulders is like television snow.

'Down by the river for what?' I ask, motivated by I do not know what magic power.

Startled, she looks around; I draw my head back.

'You have time tonight, don't you?' Her voice sounds unperturbed; I guess she does not see me.

'Oh,' I say, wondering whom she is talking to.

'Eight o'clock tonight. I'll wait beneath the willow by the river. You must come!'

I have no idea what to say.

'Why don't you answer?'

I hold my breath.

'I know what you're thinking.'

'What?'

'You're still thinking about that. OK, I'll do whatever you say.'

'What did I say?'

'Don't pretend!' she shouts. 'Why don't you come see me anymore?'

'I, I …'

'You're with someone else!' She gets hysterical.

'It's not like that,' I answer with a man's logic, curious why she cannot tell a woman's voice from a man's.

'Baby! Baby!' she screams.

'Lulu,' a woman calls from inside the room.

'Baby! Baby!'

I hear an old woman shout from inside. 'What nonsense are you screaming? I told you to take your medication but you didn't and now you're crazy again.'

'The baby! Little baby!' Loony Lulu bursts out crying.

'Come, come take your medication.'

'No!'

'Come, come.'

'No! No!'

'Then close the window. The rain is getting in.'

'Old bitch! You get on my nerves! Go away!'

I hear a scuffle, a slap, and a scream. Then silence.

'I give up,' the older woman sobs. 'Having you for a daughter is my curse in this life.'

The sobs abate—maybe the old woman left the room. I should leave too but my feet do not move.

Loony Lulu mumbles something I cannot make out.

After a few minutes she says, 'Did you go there and see it?'

'Go where and see what?'

'Next building ground floor. So tiny, cries like a cat.'

'The baby?'

'You have to promise.'

'Promise what?'

'Promise you'll never be with her again. You're with me, only me—like before!'

'I promise,' I reply, fearing another outburst might bring the old woman back in.

I have to get out of here. Once Loony Lulu discovers the promise is broken she will be devastated. I feel afraid. I make my escape not daring to look inside as I slink past the window.

'Don't forget,' her voice repeats. 'Eight o'clock tonight. I'll wait for you beneath the willow by the river.'

20

That evening after dinner I tell Ray about the 15-percent cut but not about Loony Lulu. When she spoke a thought crossed my mind. Impossible, I told myself.

Ray insists I return the money. 'It's shady—don't risk trouble.'

'Not to worry,' I say despite inward anxiety.

'It's your problem—you have to solve it yourself.'

He returns to his laptop saying he has a tight deadline. I turn on the television, skip from channel to channel listlessly, and turn it off. From the living room I pace to the bedroom and back, go into the bathroom to apply a face mask, return to the living room, and lie down on the couch.

'What happened? Still want to keep the money?'

'No, it's not that.'

Absorbed in his work he does not press me.

No matter how hard I try to banish the thought from my mind it creeps back stubbornly and stays put. The more I think about what Loony Lulu said the more insidious it seems—whether it is a good or bad omen I cannot tell.

I get up, walk to the bathroom, peel off the face mask, wash my face, apply night cream, and return to the living room. I pick up my cell phone and walk out into the backyard.

'Who lived on the ground floor of building number eleven?' I ask my aunt when she picks up.

'Why start that again? Still nosing into how the cricket book got here?'

'No, I'll tell you later. Who lived on the ground floor of building number eleven?'

'When do you mean?'

'I'm not sure.'

'Only our family and Wizard's. Who else? We moved in around 1970 or 1971. No idea who was there before that. After we moved out in 1988 Old Li's family moved in. You know them.'

I compute mentally: in 1970 Loony Lulu was a young girl, by 1988 the river was filled in. What she raves on about must have happened while my aunt's family still lived there.

'Nobody else? No tenants, relatives, friends? No young women?'

'So many years ago. Who can remember? Aunt Mira spent holidays there keeping your cousin company.' She cannot stop calling my mother Aunt Mira.

Mira. I repeat the name silently. The thought that crossed my mind this afternoon is the dark sky before a thunderstorm.

Thunderstorms burst suddenly on my childhood summers. Before the rain poured the air had a cool earthy smell, the wind blew violently, and the sky turned from yellow to dark green. My nanny came by to help take clothes in from outside and shut the windows. Thunder and lightning crashed when she left. The trees shook and flowerpots fell from upstairs, bursting in our backyard. I went to my cousin's room. On her table a book was always open and a lamp lit next to it. Everything seemed tranquil. It was only then that I thought my cousin looked pretty. Her round face was gentle and serene, comely like a Buddha. We sat side by side on the edge of her bed while she told me stories about my mother.

My mother was her best friend, she said. Everyone liked her because she was so beautiful. Before she arrived everyone in the twenty-four buildings thought Lulu was the prettiest girl around. But once they saw my mother they changed their minds. Though she was only an occasional guest she met many people—more than my cousin met in her whole life. Boys adored her. They followed her around furtively, whispering comments. The few brave ones who dared approach she chatted with ingenuously. My cousin said she looked forward to my mother pushing her around the twenty-four buildings in her wheelchair. Only then was she proud and confident. My mother was a good person, she said. Despite her beauty she never despised a cripple. She was also brave, fearing neither strangers nor darkness nor thunderstorms. Fearing nothing she was happy.

Now, thirty years on, I realize the love enemy Loony Lulu denounced was not just any woman—it was my mother; the baby she went on about was not just any infant—it was me; and the man I impersonated when I talked to her was not just any man—it was my father. How bizarre it all seems.

Quizzed by my aunt I report what Loony Lulu said.

'You believe that lunatic?' Hearing me out, she laughs—half angry, half distraught. 'Are you mad? You really believe what that lunatic told you?'

'Whether I believe her doesn't matter. What matters is what I don't know about the past and want to clear up.'

'So what if you clear it up?'

'I'll be at peace.'

'Peace? You're so naïve! These accounts are settled—there's closure at last. But now you open old wounds. You make trouble where there's no trouble anymore. What's peaceful about that?'

'I think it all has to do with my father.'

The other end of the line goes silent and a few seconds later I hear sobs.

'You don't belong in this world,' she says between sobs. 'You're illegitimate. Nobody wanted you or cared if you lived or died ...'

The sobs get louder, the talking stops.

I wait a minute or two for her to calm down.

'I understand your feelings.' She clears her throat. 'But listen to what an elder knows—what happened in the past means nothing now.'

I keep silent.

'It's all fate—once you accept it you can relax and see the future open before you.'

'You really don't know who my father is?'

'No we don't.'

'Does the cricket book have anything to do with him?'

'No.'

'Does Loony Lulu have anything to do with him?'

'Another piece of advice: the past is past; be grateful you live now.'

Hearing no reply she continues: 'Let it be. Don't let that lunatic drive you crazy. Go to bed now.'

'OK, good night.'

She hangs up.

There is something to what she says, I agree. But my thoughts are out of control and go back to the 1970s again and again. I conjure up people from thirty and forty years ago—Loony Lulu, my parents, Jianguo, Blind. Each time I think about them they seem real but the reality is fictional. Day and night feel reversed—daytime I am timid like a mouse hiding silently from the light in a corner; nighttime I cannot fall asleep recalling images from the past as if suffering obsessive-compulsive disorder.

I think to consult Brother Jin. He alone does not mind recalling the past. But how can I open up? He will laugh at my weakness and stupidity. No matter how bitter the past he can always discuss it freely. He is a strange combination of historical materialist and gambler. Past and present are two clinking dice he holds in his fingers, throws, and creates a future with. I in contrast cannot master the present much less the past or the future. I dare not expose my ineptitude. I see myself in childhood: people talked about my illicit parents deliberately within earshot. I felt angry at them but angrier at myself—I hated myself for letting them denigrate me like a mouse or a mosquito. My sole impulse was to hide far away at the end of the world.

I start to avoid Brother Jin.

Loony Lulu, however, becomes more inviting. She is the only one I am not afraid of and I know she holds the truth.

I decide to confront her again.

The next day I find an excuse to step out of the office. I take a taxi to the twenty-four buildings. My timing is bad: last time it was raining and few people were on the street; now it is overcast and many people are out. But I do not want to wait on the weather—if I do she may forget the sound of my voice. I walk up to her window quickly. Nobody is around and her room is quiet. I guess she is in the bathroom so I pretend to take a stroll through the neighborhood. When I get back a few minutes later she is still not there. Is she napping, I wonder, or ill?

People walk past me glancing curiously. I cannot hang around like this so I go back to the office.

Ray will be late this evening: he has a business dinner. I hesitate whether to try my luck with Loony Lulu again. I wait till nine and decide to go for it. I put on a windbreaker and Pumas. If I delay any longer she will be asleep when I get there.

It is foggy outside. Even with the windbreaker on I feel the damp cold in my bones. Two dim yellow headlights shine through the fog and stop in front of me. A taxi driver sticks his head out the window and asks if I need a ride. I get in.

To avoid rousing Loony Lulu I get out fifty meters from her window and walk. The sidewalk is vacant. Its sound-activated lamps are off. I step loudly so the lamps light up. When I reach her apartment I walk softly so they shut off. I stand in the dark outside the window and hear noises in the gutter—probably mice. A dim lamp illuminates her room but I see no one there. The television is off. The room is quiet and lonely. I can almost smell the dandruff on her shoulders.

The telephone rings.

Startled, I step back.

An old woman hurries in and picks up.

'Yes?' she says anxiously. From her voice I guess she is the same old woman Loony Lulu argued with yesterday.

I have no idea what she hears from the other end. Saying nothing she hangs up, gives a heavy sigh, and leaves the room.

All quiet again.

My feet freezing, I stand still and dare not turn around lest I get sucked into the fog. At last I summon the courage, take a deep breath, count to three, turn around and run. Streetlamps flare as I go past.

21

The next day after work Brother Jin is elated and invites me to dinner.

'Long time no talk,' he says. 'Just signed a big contract—don't have to drum up new business next year!'

We leave the office. He leads, I follow.

'How've you been lately?'

'OK.'

'On my end it's crazy—it never rains, it pours. But with this contract signed I can catch my breath. Ever had Manchurian food?'

I shake my head.

'You said you don't like foreign food. Tonight we'll have homegrown country food.'

'Fine.'

'No news?'

'No.'

'No news is good news.' He stops. 'Don't miss the only authentic Manchurian food in Shanghai.'

I look up and see a door to what looks like a street-level apartment. A sign above it says: BLACK EARTH.

The restaurant, no bigger than a small dining room, has four square-meter tables. Three are occupied—one by yuppies with a foreign counterpart, two by families with three generations represented. Brother Jin says it is a mom-and-pop business. The wife was a Shanghai Red Guard in Manchuria, the husband is from there.

Seeing us enter, a short, stout matron with dyed yellowish hair walks up and exchanges rapid-fire pleasantries with Brother Jin. She asks why his wife and daughter are not here, giving me a sidelong glance. He introduces us: 'This is Jianhua's younger sister; she helps at work.'

While I scan the menu for something light Brother Jin orders Manchurian bean curd salad, string beans stir-fried with pickles, and roasted pig's face.

Even the words upset my stomach. I try to protest but he says, 'When I was a Red Guard in Manchuria these were delicacies we could enjoy only at Chinese New Year's.'

He summons the matron: 'A bottle of liquor!' and continues, 'I don't know why I never felt full back then no matter how much I ate. Like a pig I thought all day long about eating. I could eat ten steamed buns at a time, probably because we lacked animal fat. I could eat my fill only at Chinese New Year's—so I yearned for it all year long.'

A man at the next table overhears and pipes in: 'Ah, old comrade from Manchuria! Chinese New Year's was really fun in the countryside back then—drag a pig out and slaughter it right there with people crowding round, all beating the metal washbasins they used to collect meat slices. You'd say whatever cut you liked and how much and the butcher would slice it off exactly right. A Red Guard brother got excited to tears seeing a warm slaughtered pig and screamed he wanted to eat raw meat. The butcher thought he was joking and tossed him a bloody slice. He caught it with both hands and bolted it without blinking.'

'Old fool! Why tell the girl that? She won't understand,' the matron says, arriving at our table with a roasted pig's head on a platter.

Brother Jin hands me a pair of cellophane gloves. Following his example I roll up my sleeves, pull the gloves on, tear off a chunk of well-roasted pig's face, put it on my plate, remove the gloves, and eat it with chopsticks. It is too greasy—I cannot get more than a few bites down.

'Delicious, isn't it?' The matron arrives with the two other dishes. 'Eat as much as you like. What you can't finish I'll pack up and take next door: the couple there were also Red Guards in Manchuria but are now unemployed; life's hard for them. We bring them food every day. Things like pig's face and lamb's bones served with gloves they think hygienic. Other leftovers they won't touch.'

She pulls up a chair and joins us. 'When we were sent to the countryside I was the youngest in my class—only fourteen. When the train left Shanghai station everyone cried except me. Why cry if I could still see my family again? Innocently I arrived in Manchuria. Another girl and I were set on a donkey cart and taken to a nearby village. The peasant driving asked where we were from. We said Shanghai. He asked why Shanghai people would ever come there. We said it was fun. He said little did we know—it was no fun at all.'

'Saying it's fun makes it fun, saying it's no fun makes it no fun,' the same man at the next table remarks. 'Life was hard but not unbearable. If you ask me we were happier then than teenagers are now.'

Brother Jin nods emphatically. 'Before we were sent to the countryside we traveled around China for free—free train, free food, free shelter. Great fun! Remember?'

'I was still young,' the matron says, 'just a girl. My family wouldn't let me go. There was a boy of twelve next door. His older brothers and sisters all went; he demanded to go too. His mother sewed eight pockets into his underwear, putting money in each, and let him go. He came back two months later—he was robbed the first day out but could still tour the country without spending a cent.'

I feel lucky they all chat away. No one pays me any attention or notices my discomfort.

'Come, I'll take you home,' Brother Jin says outside the restaurant door.

'No need—it's close by, I can walk.'

'Then I'll walk you.'

I accept, fearing it will be suspicious if I decline twice.

'Why so quiet this evening?'

'Nothing to talk about. What you all talked about is nothing I know.'

'Something's on your mind.'

'What's on my mind?'

'How would I know?' He laughs. 'I hear you got Wizard's cricket book back.'

'Yes.'

'Where did you find it?'

'Secondhand bookstall.'

'Where?'

'Yuyuan Garden.'

'Stay clear of the cricket business—I warned you it's trouble.'

'I've got nothing to do with it now.'

'Say what's on your mind and you'll feel better.' He seems to want to make me confess. 'If you don't trust me, of course, it's another story.'

A desire to confess swells in my chest. Didn't I always want to ask him about history? I should exploit my courage before it fails.

'I spoke with the lunatic,' I say quickly.

'Who?'

'Loony Lulu in the building next to Wizard's.'

'Why talk to her?'

'To ask about my father.'

'What?'

'Perhaps you never heard I'm an orphan. I was six when I learned who my mother was but she was already dead. Now I've got a clue to my father.'

'I heard something about that from Jianhua. Good you've got a clue. You should look him up. Reunion is joyous.'

'I don't know how to find him.'

'Didn't you say you had a clue?'

'It's hard to believe ...'

'Nothing's hard to believe.'

Comforted, I tell him everything Loony Lulu said exactly.

He says nothing.

'What do you think?'

'Oh?' He seems to awake from a dream.

'Should I ask Loony Lulu again? Or her mother?'

'You think they'd tell you?'

'Why not?'

'You're opening old wounds. These accounts are all settled. Why upset everyone? What's the point?' He sounds like my aunt.

I see his neck reddened with the alcohol he smells of and am put off.

'You said to look my father up.'

'Yes, but not this way. What you're doing now hurts others and doesn't help you.'

'What I've heard makes no sense, I want to know why and ...'

'And what?'

'Intuition tells me what Loony Lulu said isn't crazy.'

'Don't be silly. She's insane.'

My eyes tear. I regret telling him all this. As I feared I am inviting insult.

His tone softens. 'If you were anyone else I wouldn't care. But because you're you I want to talk you out of it. My words may hurt but I mean well. The past is past, you can't live backwards. What difference does it make if you know who your father is? You never knew who he was the last thirty years did you?'

I shake my head.

'Until a few days ago you didn't know anything but you were happy and well. How did you get like this? You're still young—you should look ahead not backward.'

I sense a conspiracy.

'Are you keeping something from me?'

'You're being ridiculous! Even your own aunt and uncle don't know so how could I? If I knew anything I'd have told you already. You're not a child anymore. Why should I hide anything from you?'

'Did you know Mira?'

'Mira?'

'Yang Shuli. They called her Mira.'

'Sounds faintly familiar but I didn't know her. Why?'

'She was my mother.'

'I should've guessed.'

'You never heard of her?'

'Not that I recall. Long ago. Who remembers?'

'You remember a lot.'

'My memory is an attic full of junk that once mattered. But your mother isn't there.'

'Tell me the truth!'

'Lay off, let it be.'

'I have to go see Loony Lulu again.'

'Go ahead. Do what you like. Nobody's stopping you.'

Joffre New Village is in the next block. I stop. 'No need to walk me any farther.'

He stops too. 'Relax, sleep well. Your mind will be clearer in the morning.'

'Bye,' I say, more depressed than I was a few hours ago.

22

In bed I think on what Brother Jin said and the more I think the more I feel wronged. Those who lived the history are hypocrites. They take the past dead seriously but tell you it is meaningless. They say they protect you but steal your right to know. Ignorance is bliss? Many people seem to think so. They think I prefer being ignorant too. When I started digging up the past they told me how awful it was. Actually they are frightened—frightened I will awake painful memories. If this is not 'plugging one's ears to silence the alarm bell,' what is it?

Early next morning at work Brother Jin summons me to his office. Little Boss is there too.

'I just spoke with Jason,' Brother Jin says. 'He'll take you along to Beijing to meet clients. I wanted you to go there earlier but one delay led to another and now you have to go quickly to beat the year-end rush.'

'When?'

'Monday morning, OK?'

I look first at him, then at Little Boss. Their expression says I had better comply. I agree to travel.

'Discuss travel details with Jason.'

'Let's meet at two this afternoon,' Little Boss says. 'Anything else?' he asks Brother Jin.

'That's it.'

Little Boss opens the door and leaves.

I start to follow but Brother Jin calls me back. 'Stay a moment.'

'Something else?'

'Let's have lunch.'

'What's left to discuss that we can't discuss now?'

'Let's have lunch. Twelve-thirty. Meet me at the Ritz Carlton Japanese restaurant.'

I arrive five minutes early. Brother Jin is on time.

'Do you know why I send you on a business trip?' he asks, sitting down.

'To divert me.'

'You're not so confused after all.'

He hands me a small purple box.

'What's this?'

'Jianhua asked me to buy it in the duty-free shop at the airport but when I gave it to her she didn't want it anymore. Keep it if you like it.'

I open the box and see a flacon of Guerlain. My anger from last night lingers. In no mood to be polite I snap the box shut and put it in my purse with no word of thanks.

'Last night you said I remembered a lot. Did Jianhua ever tell you how we met?'

I shake my head.

'The first time I saw her she was eight or nine. She tagged along with Jianguo, obviously his little sister.'

'Not a pedophile are you?'

'You've got a sick mind.'

A waitress walks up to take our order. I choose a sushi menu, Brother Jin takes the same.

'No sake?' I ask him.

'Not today, I had too much alcohol last night; better take it easy.'

The waitress leaves; he continues: 'After graduating from the worker-peasant-soldier university I stayed in Shanghai and worked at a bank. Once I went to the twenty-four buildings to do I forget what and saw Jianhua on the street. She was in high school and good-looking, better than before. She stared as if trying to recall where she knew me from; I looked back and she looked away. I won't forget that scene as long as I live. Later we ran into each other a few more times, mostly on sunny days when she helped her grandmother take a walk. Time passed but I always remembered that girl. One day while riding my bike before I went to America I got hit by a truck, broke an arm, and was brought to the hospital. The attending nurse was Jianhua. I was so surprised I thought she was a delusion brought on by the painkiller. I asked if she was Jianguo's sister. She said yes, unsurprised as if she knew I would ask.'

'How romantic.'

He smiles with satisfaction betraying nostalgia.

'During the two weeks I was in hospital I saw I also meant something to her and got brave. The day I was discharged I invited her to a movie but decided not to get involved because I was afraid to lead her on: the bank had already decided to post me abroad—I lacked work experience but was the only one they could find who spoke English well enough to do the job. The posting was for three years. I didn't want Jianhua to wait for me; I preferred to wait for her. She was young, not yet twenty.'

'What happened?'

The waitress reappears with two sushi sets on a tray.

Brother Jin eyes her smiling and says: 'I worked three years, took one more to get an MBA, and returned to Shanghai in 1987 to represent a multinational—back then people with foreign degrees got good jobs. I looked Jianhua up at the hospital; she was still there; we got involved. It all went smoothly. Came time to tell her parents I got nervous. Everyone knew Shanghai natives despised provincials. Shanghai in the 1980s was different from now. If you didn't speak Shanghai dialect or spoke it with an accent you were ignored, glared at, even insulted. Jianhua said she'd handle her parents. Probably because they saw I had money they agreed.'

'Were Wizard and my nanny so snobbish?'

'Not really—they just wanted to improve their condition like everybody else. They seemed ingenuous but were cunning. And Jianhua seemed quiet and gentle but was really tough.'

'That I can imagine.'

'I'm grateful to Jianhua. She's more daring and resolute than I am. Ten years ago I quit my job as chief representative and started my own business. Nobody else understood; only Jianhua encouraged me. Later, when the business lost money, she sold her jewelry to help. She said: "Finish what you start." Her parents found out and were hopping mad. Jianhua told me, "I'll handle my parents but you've got three years: if you can't give me a good life by then I'll divorce you." I agreed. Everything turned around before the three years were up.'

Talking slowly, leaning back in his chair, resting his hands on the table with fingers intertwined, he shows none of his aggressive ebullience. His story makes me forget what is on my mind; my anger from last night is diluted as well. I begin to understand why he invited me to lunch and will send me to Beijing on business—self-doubt consumes me as I think what he said last night may be true. I do not believe the perfume was a present Jianhua did not want but say nothing: since he apologized I can forgive. The alcoholic smell of his body is gone completely. His large hands, accentuated by pressed white cuffs, are immaculate with manicured nails. On the left ring finger a platinum wedding band shines. A man who reeks of alcohol and a man so clean and neat are night and day. Vanity, vanity, I laugh to myself.

'What's so funny?'

'Nothing. You look like Ken Takakura, that's all.'

'Is he as spirited as I am?'

'You're small eyes concentrating light, he's big eyes dispersing light.'

We laugh. When we stop he looks at me: 'You should be like this more often.'

I nod.

When I get home that evening I tell Ray I will be away for a week on a business trip. Predictably his face falls at once.

'We don't have many days left; now you're off on a business trip a whole week.'

'I'll be back soon.'

'Can't you postpone the trip till I'm gone?'

'Very difficult.'

'I'll talk to your boss.'

'No point—I want to go.'

'Why?'

'To unwind.'

'You think a business trip's relaxing?'

'Work can be a form of therapy.'

'Are you going off with a new lover?'

'I'm in no mood to argue. You're the one who insists on leaving me for America.'

His face turns sullen. 'You're still on my case. I thought we already agreed.'

I want to tell him what happened the last few days but suppress it. He would never understand.

'Yes we agreed. I'm not on your case,' I say, knowing my hypocrisy—how could I not care?

'OK, if you want to go, go. But when you're back you're mine.'

'Deal.'

'Don't renege.'

'I won't.'

He smiles naughtily.

Though I agreed with Brother Jin not to dwell on the past, morbid thoughts crowd my mind as I lie awake in bed. Looking at Ray sound asleep next to me, I think it best not to tell him. For now he is my refuge through long nights—waiting for dawn I have no one else to cling to.

I hesitate several days then decide to make one last attempt to debrief Loony Lulu. If I get nothing this time I will give up.

I reach the twenty-four buildings Sunday afternoon at ten before two. Fearing Loony Lulu's family will refuse me, I go to the local community office to ask for a meeting. The office is completely different now from when I was a child. Outside the gate there is no public telephone or convenience store, only a condom dispenser with a sign pasted on it saying: BIRTH CONTROL. Inside the office there are no retired matron volunteers anymore, only young professional civil servants. The festive gongs, drums, and big red paper flowers that used to rest against the wall are replaced by a newspaper shelf and a public computer.

'What do you want?' a young woman asks, standing up behind a desktop computer.

'I used to live here in building eleven and want to ask the people in building ten, apartment 101, about old family business. But I don't know them personally. Could you introduce us?'

'Family business? No need to go through this office.'

'May I trouble you to put us in touch?'

She opens an Excel sheet on the computer, picks up the telephone expressionlessly, and dials a number.

She holds the receiver for half a minute, puts it down, and says, 'No answer.'

'I'll come back in half an hour.'

I leave the office and walk toward Wizard's. From a distance, approaching Loony Lulu's, I see a crowd. Getting closer I hear hysterical wails and shouts. 'My daughter, why such a miserable fate? Without you—my curse from the previous life—I can now die in peace!' I squeeze through the crowd and see an old woman sitting on the ground—her hair disheveled, face wet with tears and snot, forehead bruised and abraded.

'What happened?' I ask a man next to me.

'The cops said they found a decomposing corpse in a smelly creek outside the city. What was she doing out there?'

'Her crazy daughter went missing the other night,' another man adds. 'The cops asked her just now to identify the body. It's probably her daughter—they're not often wrong about things like that.'

My ears buzz, my stomach churns: I vomit on the sidewalk and glimpse bits of the pizza I ate for lunch. People around me jump back half a meter.

'Yuck! Can't you barf someplace else?'

Loony Lulu kept her appointment by the river that night. The man she went there to meet was my elusive father. Am I a matchmaker who sent her to my father or a demon who sent her to her death?

'What happened?' someone asks in a voice that sounds distant and dreamy.

I shake my head. My stomach is convulsed from guilt or terror, I do not know which.

I want to raze the twenty-four buildings, dig up all secrets buried in the mildewy mud, and expose them to the sunlight.

But now, Sunday afternoon at two with sunlight shining on my head, I try to cover my face with my jacket collar. I hate my weakness and hypocrisy; I lack even courage to face the sunlight.

Another onlooker speaks like an offscreen voice in a movie: 'Death is not such a bad thing. What's the point of her going on living like that?'

'Not a bad thing, not a bad thing …' I repeat silently. In my mind's eye I see a pale swollen face like a steamed bun soaked in water that disintegrates into gooey fragments at a touch.

Retribution

23

The northern air dries out my mildewy mind. In this week away I think many things through and decide to call off the search. Maybe everyone is right that dark memories are best forgotten. Maybe Loony Lulu's disaster was not death but thirty years of delusion. Maybe we remember happiness and forget sorrow to survive. Maybe we have to respect this basic instinct. Maybe it is the right attitude toward life. I want to forget everything. I want to forget about the spring of 1976 and the eyes staring at me from a tombstone. I want to forget the yellowed cricket book and Wizard's opaque tears. I want to forget the drowned lunatic, my untimely dead mother, and my anonymous father. I do not want to talk about any of it. I just want to be like everyone else and live with immediate worry not distant anxiety.

Little Boss and I dash from one business meeting to another by day and attend business dinners at night. Only in the taxi from place to place do we get a chance to talk. He says he will leave the company early next year but will not go back to Singapore—maybe Bangkok or Kuala Lumpur, he is not sure. He says he resigned but I sense he holds a grudge. I ask what happened. He says he has been in China too long and wants a change of scene: 'I'm from the tropics and will go back there.'

He laughs and after a pause says, 'Don't stay with the company too long. People are inertial. Before you're married with children you should find a better place to grow.'

'You mean it's a bad place to work?'

'The staff is good but the management is not.'

'What's wrong?'

'No transparency, distrust of subordinates.'

'You mean Big Boss?'

'Best I say no more.'

'I heard complaints about him too.'

'Draw your own conclusions.'

Little Boss is always careful. That he said so much is most unusual. I recall gossip I heard about Brother Jin being selfish and despotic, arrogant and stubborn, ruthless, susceptible to flattery, involved with Nancy … I never took it seriously and thought it must be motivated by fear and envy. But hearing Little Boss today I begin to wonder because he seems direct and sincere. People complain he is a workaholic but respect him and never gossip maliciously at his expense.

On second thought, however, the clash between Little Boss and Brother Jin could be personality or a power struggle. Who the good and bad guy are is unclear. I trust intuition—when I met Brother Jin we clicked like old friends. Despite our disagreement I sense something special that attracts me—I do not believe intuition can go far wrong.

When I return from the business trip it is already November. The northern cold follows me south. A hard chill pervades Shanghai. Ray leaves for America in a week. He never mentions it or asks whether I will join him. If he insists I might waver but he does not; I never felt so dependent. When not at work I follow him everywhere. With him I live in a dream world of pristine sweetness with all darkness and morbidity expunged. There is no past, future, memory, or expectation—only serenity here and now.

Ray's friends decide to throw him a good-bye party. They schedule it for 7 November, the night before he takes off.

'Why didn't you save the last night for us?' I ask.

'I wish I could've but had to accept majority rule. My flight isn't till the next evening anyway—we'll have the whole day to ourselves.'

Ray and I agree to host the party at my place so we can decide whom to invite and exclude. Ray invites most guests; I invite some friends as well. We invite twenty between us but more show up, mostly strangers.

When Linda walks in she shouts to me: 'I invited you over for dinner but you never came. Your loss. Now I can party all I want!'

She brings several bottles of wine and a few noisy unattached women her age.

'Knock yourself out,' I say. 'It's been a while.'

Ray is the DJ. Dressed in a tight black T-shirt, black denims, black-rimmed glasses, and a black driver's cap, he sits connecting an amplifier and speakers to his laptop in a corner of the living room.

'Who's this foreign hunk?' I hear one girl from the office ask another.

'He's hot!'

I did not want to include them but they overheard me invite Amy.

'What party?' they asked, pretending not to know. 'Can we come too?'

'Of course,' I faked a smile. 'You're welcome.'

I guess they have no idea Ray is my boyfriend. They may

even dream of being his girlfriend and running off with him to some faraway country. I feel proud and sad.

The party starts at eight; the Jin family arrives at nine. Ting and Jianhua walk arm in arm like sisters, each with a Hermès purse on her elbow. This is the first time I see Ting. Like her father she is tall—half a head taller than Jianhua—but has her mother's delicate features.

They sit and chat till half past ten, then get set to leave. Ting wants to stay but her parents say, 'It's late, you've got school tomorrow.'

She pouts and fusses like a child; Brother Jin gives in. 'OK, we'll stay another half-hour.'

'Another half-hour? Maybe you don't have to sleep but I do,' Jianhua says.

'You two go home, I'll be there later,' Ting says.

'No way—forget it,' Jianhua replies.

'OK, OK,' Brother Jin says. 'Let her stay out late for once. I'll pick her up in an hour.'

'So now it's an hour?' Jianhua glares at him.

Meeting Big Boss socially, the office girls lose all timidity. One of them, nudged forward by another, asks with a naughty smile, 'Big Boss, may we come to work a bit late tomorrow?'

'Ten latest.'

'Thanks!' They flutter off like birds.

'This boss and father can't refuse anyone,' Jianhua says walking to the door. Brother Jin follows.

At the door Jianhua grabs both my hands: 'Fun like this is OK now and then but don't make it a habit. I know young people back from abroad like to party but it's no good for your body. I have to be in bed by eleven every night. Eleven to three is the body's prime time to cleanse and regenerate. If you're not asleep then you can sleep all day and it won't help. You're past thirty—take care of your body. Maybe people can't see now but whether a woman takes care of herself is written on her face a few years later. Today is the beginning of winter. You should eat chicken soup made with dates and wolfberries and get to bed early. Seeing iced drinks and alcohol late at night scares me. It's getting cold, mind your body.'

Brother Jin tugs her sleeve. 'Didn't you say you belong in bed?'

Jianhua turns to me: 'Take care of yourself.'

A friend of Ray's arrives with his pregnant wife. I order all smokers out into the backyard. Ray has the laptop play jazz over and over. Guests cluster in small groups, sitting on chairs or leaning drowsily against each other on the couch.

'It's getting on eleven,' I tell Ray. 'Play dance music.'

He returns to the laptop. A few seconds later a loud thump-thump beat fills the room. Startled, the guests catch on—they cavort to the music and glow with excitement. Ting gambols ecstatically like Cinderella racing the clock to midnight. Smokers in the backyard hear the music and, extinguishing their cigarettes, crowd in.

'The ball started and no one told me,' Linda beefs.

One of her girlfriends, obviously drunk, swills wine from a bottle and moves against the music not with it.

In the rush no one closes the backdoor. Cold wind jets in. I shiver, walk over to close the door, and see two unfamiliar Chinese guys in the backyard.

'No idea what a white girl is like in bed,' one says to the other. 'Want to give it a try?'

'Damn, you've got a big appetite. You don't even speak English. How can you expect to get one?'

'No need to talk, just get it on,' I say leaning on the door-frame.

They chortle obscenely.

Returning from the backyard to the living room, I feel my eardrums vibrate and the floor shake—I fear the ceiling may cave in. Is Ray's amplifier that strong? Is he trying to outdo Red Regime? Tonight he is drunk.

I try to turn it down when Amy walks up and shouts something in my ear I cannot make out. She shouts again but I still cannot understand. I pull her outside and ask what she said.

'Three guys I don't know just walked in. Go look. Did you invite them?'

I step back inside and see three foreign guys standing in the corner. Each holds a bottle of Bacardi Breezer. They brought their own.

I pull Ray outside. 'Did you invite these jokers?'

'No.'

'Are they Linda's friends?'

'No, crashers.'

Now I remember I left the door unlocked so Brother Jin could get back in but when he left with Ting I forgot to lock it.

'Don't worry,' Ray says, sensing my anxiety. 'I had a chat—they're OK, they're students. They couldn't find Red Regime and followed their ears here.'

'Turn that shit off!' a neighbor shouts. 'Some people have to sleep so they can work for a living.'

We say nothing.

'Fuck your mother!' I hear the same voice. 'As if the night-club down the street isn't bad enough. Now we've got one here too. Fuck your mother!'

His curse splits the night. Several windows light up. One opens. I tell Ray to kill the music right now.

'Fuck your mother! Can't you hear? Turn that shit off or I'll call the police!'

We slip back inside. Ray turns down the volume and tells me to shut the windows tight.

'That's it,' I shout. 'Party's over.'

'It's early,' Ray says. 'We're grooving now.'

'What if he calls the cops?'

'Who turned down the music?' a crasher asks.

'OK, everybody out—party's over.' I shut the music off. 'A neighbor's calling the cops.'

'He's bluffing,' Ray says.

Someone turns the music back on.

'Don't mind the neighbor,' Linda says. 'Keep dancing.'

I turn the music off again.

'Is this my place or what?' I glare at Ray.

The girls from the office walk up and say it is late, they have to go. Others glance at each other for cues what to do. Several propose to leave. They say goodbye in turn. Twenty minutes later only Ray, Linda, her friends, and I remain. Linda and her friends, alert to any opportunity for fun, say it is too hot inside and step out into the backyard to cool off. I fear their chatter will provoke the neighbor so I coax them back inside.

'It's snowing,' the drunk girl says.

I suspect pink elephants but see it really is snowing—at first thin, light, fragile, and beguiling, then dense and heavy.

'Come look, it's snowing!' I pull Ray outside.

'It's only November: how come it's snowing?' asks one of Linda's friends.

'The weather's unseasonable,' Ray says. 'Last week it was

twenty degrees, tonight it's snowing. Global warming.'

'Unseasonable weather is a bad omen,' I say.

'Who cares?' Linda says. 'We've got snow—enjoy it.'

24

The apartment seems especially empty now the party is over; the smell of alcohol lingers. Ray lies next to me snoring gently. Memories invade in the quiet void of night.

As a child I went to bed every night at eight. Because I would not share a room with my cousin my aunt put a foldout bed in the hall and spread a clean sheet and quilt over it. In the dim light I often took a long time to fall asleep. One side of the bed was bright, the other dark. The bright side was illuminated by street lamps outside the kitchen window. The dark side was near the two closed bedroom doors. The theme song of a Japanese soap opera came through the door of my aunt and uncle's room. Sometimes one of them came out to get a glass of water and asked why I was still awake. My cousin never came out. I never knew when my eyes closed, only that it was suddenly morning.

Those were the happy nights. There were others when nightmares possessed me. The week after my mother's funeral they came every night. Then I slept alongside my aunt in her big bed. Her bedroom had a second door that opened into the backyard. That door had a window in the top half covered by a small curtain. On a bright night the moonlight cast shadows on the curtain. The more I looked the more they resembled my mother's waxen face. I buried my head in the quilt and held my aunt's hand. When I fell asleep my mother's ghost pursued me. I dreamed of her sometimes by the river, sometimes at the pancake stand, sometimes in the rural wilderness, and once in the wartime pillbox. I would wake with a jolt and sit up, soaked in sweat. My aunt would press me back down on the bed, hold me in her arms, and sing lullabies: 'Row, row, row to Grandma Bridge … Row, row, row to Golden Water Bridge.'

Tonight I lie in bed staring at the curtain again. Ever since I saw my mother's waxen face at her funeral I could not recall what she really looked like. To recall her real face I had to rely on photos. But when I stared at the images they became lifeless and the ghostly visage came back. I turn on my side, hug Ray from behind, and press my face to his neck. I close my eyes but the waxen face is still there. I know resistance is futile—I can only hug my lover tight and wait for dawn.

Jianhua may be right: do not party, have a quiet dinner, retire early, enjoy pillow talk, make love, go to sleep contented. To spend our last night that way would make more sense.

Half asleep I see my nanny's living room. She smiles from the black frame on the wall; Wizard carves holes in taros at the table. It is dark, lights off, curtains open. Snow in the backyard reflects moonlight, coloring the taros violet. Crickets in the hollow taros chirp feebly, waiting for death. Terror seizes me. Tonight's unseasonable snow is ominous. Will something befall Wizard? I see a shrunken dark old man lying on a worn-out floor; next to him in the darkness rows of taros emit faint cold light.

I want to call Wizard but the time is awkward. If he is all right I shall be embarrassed. I toss in bed, waiting for the eastern sky to turn white. Ray extends his arm to hold me still. Two or three hours were never so long. I count silently from one to sixty over and over again—if I do it more than a hundred twenty times dawn will break.

When I wake up it is bright outside; I have no idea how long I slept. Ray is still asleep. I get up, make myself a cup of coffee, put on a jacket, and go into the backyard. It is very cold. I quickly retreat to put on a sweater before stepping outside again. The snow, neither piled up nor melted, is soggy like sherbet left out at room temperature. I kick some snow and feel my sock get wet inside my shoe. Winter is here again. I hate winter in Shanghai. It may not be so cold but if you stand still outside for five minutes you get chilled to the bone.

I check my cell phone. Six-thirty. Wizard should be up by now. I wonder how to ask my question. I cannot tell him I want to check whether he is alive, but this is no time to fuss about protocol. What if something bad happened?

The phone rings four or five times. Wizard answers.

I sigh with relief and smile. 'I just remembered—how's General Guan doing?'

'Ah, General Guan.' He draws the name out slowly. 'Died last night.'

'How do you know?'

'I can hear. Even if they're in taros I can hear.'

'Hope it had a good journey.'

'Attained nirvana,' he mutters. 'Nirvana.'

I feel much better knowing Wizard is OK. Last night's morbid thoughts are gone. I go back to bed and lie next to Ray. I try to nap but when my eyes open the sun is high and bright. Ray sits at the table staring into his laptop. His luggage stands against the wall.

'I was afraid you'd sleep through our last day.'

'What time is it?'

'Twelve.'

I get up, walk over to Ray, shut his laptop, and escort him back to bed.

'We'll skip lunch today.'

We spend the next three hours making love. I do not know where or when I can see him again. The room is temperate. Sunlight filters through the curtains and yellows our bodies. It feels like the first weekend I spent with him—life in a bubble out of time. But our reverie ends abruptly. We have to get a taxi at four for him to catch the plane at seven.

'You can always change your mind,' he says in the taxi.

'I know.'

'Will you?'

'Maybe.'

'You're the stubbornest person I ever met.'

'You're stubborn too.' Our amorous exertions leave me emotionally as well as physically sore. 'Who's happier—the one who starts a new life or the one who stays put?'

'That depends on their lives.'

'What about you and me?'

'The first week will be hard but later we'll both have it easier.'

'The question is who'll forget first.'

'You'll forget first.'

'No, you will.'

'Want to bet?'

'How much?'

'Dinner at a Michelin three-star restaurant.'

'Deal. When?'

'This time next year. What day is it?'

'It's 8 November. How can you forget the date on your ticket?'

'How do we arrange it?'

'If you win you come here and I treat. If I win I go there and you treat.'

'You mean the winner has to pay the plane fare?'

'To get anything you have to give up something else.'

We continue like this—half joking, half serious—all the way to the airport by the sea. Frivolous banter does not soothe the hurt. At every pause in conversation I feel an invisible hand grab my heart, yank it up to my throat, and push it back to my chest.

Time is short. Ray goes straight to check his luggage and get his boarding pass. Rolled-up in kraft paper, the Cultural Revolution posters he bought stick out of his backpack.

I walk with him through the waiting area before passport control, slowing our pace.

'Want a drink?' he asks.

'You'd better get through passport control. Don't want to miss your plane.'

'OK.'

We stop at the entry point between two stainless steel fences where two policemen stand guard.

Ray lays his hand on my head and says, 'Don't forget our bet.'

'I won't if you don't.'

Ignoring the gaze of other passengers, he gives me a long French kiss and steps between the policemen to the other side.

I cry like a child. He does not turn around.

The shuttle bus moves haltingly through rush-hour traffic. I do not care. Washed by snow the sky is clear and bright. Venus appears. Countless buildings line the route; countless lights illuminate the buildings; countless people crowd the sidewalks. Neon lights shine on their faces—all look happy.

Passengers get off the bus stop by stop. It gets emptier and emptier. Absentmindedly I reach the end of the line.

'Show your ticket,' the conductor says.

I hand it to her.

'Not full fare. You should've gotten off two stops ago. That's twenty yuan extra. Pay up.'

I see I missed my stop and pay without argument.

I catch a taxi home. The driver takes a shortcut past a row of family restaurants. The aroma of food and liquor overwhelms me. I remember I ate nothing all day and am famished at once. The fridge at home is empty; I ask the driver to stop.

I choose a quiet restaurant and order a bowl of noodle soup. Eating alone is no fun. I finish the soup quickly, pay, and leave. With my hunger appeased my mood improves. Animality runs deep.

25

When the next taxi I catch arrives at Joffre New Village I change my mind. I know I must face an empty apartment but lack the courage and ask the driver to take me to the South Ocean Hotel instead.

Once there I go straight to Mask. Inside a dozen yuppies are having a party. Several girls push a guy to the bar and threaten to pour liquor down his throat. His booming laugh sets off their shrill giggles. Their eyes brim with pride as if the whole world envied their youth and success.

The garden terrace is closed for winter; the bar is packed with couples and businesspeople. It got the nickname South Ocean Brothel because of a large mahogany bed against one wall.

Several men and women recline on the bed. Red lantern light filters through a peachy pink gauze net, coloring their faces rosy. Next to the bed is a mahogany tea table with a candle and ashtray on top. The candleholder looks like an opium lamp, the ashtray like an opium bowl. Now and then people on the bed wriggle over to sip drinks from glasses on the tea table and wriggle back again. There is no place for me on the bed and all tables are occupied. I make a lap around the room and take a stool at the bar.

'Gin and tonic,' I tell the bartender, and notice the guy in sunglasses paying up next to me is the one I saw my first night back in Shanghai.

'Jianjun?'

He smiles, moves behind me from left to right, and takes a bar stool. 'You must be Lan.'

'Why change places?'

He shakes his head, dismissing the question. 'Never thought I'd run into you here.'

'Quite a coincidence.'

'I meant to look you up but couldn't find time.'

'No problem. You're busy with business.'

'Good we met here. I have to fly south tomorrow morning. Don't know when I'll be back.'

'It's good being busy. Business must prosper.'

'You're alone?'

'Just saw a friend off at the airport. You're here by yourself?'

'Just finished doing business with a client.'

The bartender sets a gin and tonic in front of me.

'A Coke,' Jianjun tells him. It seems he wants to chat.

'Why only Coke?'

'I have to drive.'

I sip the gin and tonic. 'Thanks for the 15 percent. A lot of money but I can't take it.'

'You already did—keep it.'

'I took it because I can't argue with Wizard. I want to return it but had no chance to see you.'

'Don't be silly. Take every chance you get to make money. If you don't these days you starve.'

'Banks are closed. Come back from the south and I'll give it to you.'

'Don't bother.'

'When do you get back?'

'Don't bother, I mean it.'

'No, *I* mean it.'

'I don't know if I'll ever come back … Kidding!' he says before I can reply. 'General Guan's the best damned cricket I ever saw—won a million in three matches. What a fighter!'

Jianjun's sunglasses, light brown in the barroom light, expose the corner of his left eye. Memory is instant. The face is the one I knew—oval shape, prominent chin, lion nose, peach-flower mouth—except the eyes are shaded. Behind the sunglasses his left eye looks normal. The right one must be blind—hence his move to my right. What does his blind eye look like? Dark hollow or dirty gelatin?

'Did you see the cricket book I gave Wizard?'

'Yes, very kind and thoughtful, thank you.'

'I found it by accident. Nothing to thank me for.'

'Oh yes there is. If you hadn't found it I would've blamed myself the rest of my life.'

'Why?'

'I didn't know any better and had a big mouth, telling everyone we had an occult book at home. Bad guys stole it.'

'Blind and his gang?'

'You know?'

'I heard.'

'You're something—even know about Blind.'

'Wizard said a gang of kids stole the book—I guessed it was Blind.'

'Blind,' he mutters. 'That day I was napping at home and heard someone in the living room demand the "poisonous weed." Then bigger kids pushed into the bedroom, Blind in front. They turned it upside down; a few ransacked the bathroom and kitchen. I was too scared to cry. Later I knew it was my fault. After losing the book my family couldn't eat or sleep—bad things happened to us. They said it was punishment from our ancestors.'

'May I ask you something?'

'Why so polite?'

'Did the cricket book have anything to do with Jianguo getting killed?'

'You know about my brother too?'

'I heard.'

'How come you know so much? Who told you?'

'Brother Jin.'

'Him? Since when is it his fucking business?'

'I asked him.'

'Sly old fox!'

'You don't get on?'

'Thanks to him I lost an eye.'

'I heard you lost it fighting over a cricket.'

'Yeah—with him.'

'He played crickets too?'

'Played? Don't make me laugh. He invented it.'

'You mean he stole your cricket and beat you up?'

'He didn't do it himself; he was behind it.'

'Then why is he your family's son-in-law?'

'He told lies so good they could raise the dead. My family believed him not me. What a load!'

'A face can hide a mind.'

'Tell me about it. I accept bad fortune, OK? But you know what he did? When I was locked up he pretended to spring me. What did he have except dirty money? All he spent to get me out I paid back with interest. His money isn't worth shit now. Japan, America—their economies are down. He's keeping up appearances. I'm richer than he is so he's ashamed to see me. That's just fine.'

Taking sides is unwise—I keep silent.

He swills the Coke. 'If you didn't despise people like me I could give you a job. I can pay more than he does.'

'I don't despise you.'

'I'm no fool.'

Seeing me embarrassed and irritated, he opens a way out. 'Let's talk about something else. Where were we?'

'I asked if the cricket book had anything to do with your brother's death.'

'Good guess. My brother went after Blind because of that book.'

'And the gang war? Also because of the book?'

He nods. 'Seriously, nobody knows I caused it all. At first I told no one because I was afraid. Later nobody mentioned it anymore so I let it go.'

'Maybe it's better to let things go.'

'Easy to say. As long as the subject never comes up it's OK. But when it does I get upset.'

'You were still a kid then. How could anyone blame you?'

'I told myself that too but my heart won't rest. Am I weak?'

'Not at all. You have a good heart.'

'A good heart isn't worth shit. But drop it. I just want to say you earned your 15 percent. It's what I owe you.'

'The bad things already happened. I found the book too late.'

'Never too late: the cricket book is the family amulet—from now on our ancestors will bless us with peace and harmony.' He joins his hands together as if in prayer.

'The book was at my aunt and uncle's all along.'

'What?'

'It was in my cousin's room. When my uncle removed her effects he sold it to a bookshop downtown. From there it went to a book stall in Yuyuan Garden where I found and bought it for Wizard.'

'Cripple? How did she get it?'

'We don't know—nobody does. Maybe Blind left it with her.'

'No way. What did he have to do with her? Mira must've left it there.'

'Who?'

'The pretty woman at your aunt's place every summer who died. I don't remember much except that she was next door and wore a blouse with a bunch of grapes printed on it. She was kind to me. I didn't know much about anything then but I always liked her.'

'You mean Blind gave her the book?'

'Probably. She was close to Blind's gang.'

'What?'

'She was Commander's girlfriend. As a kid I sneaked out at night to catch crickets with friends. One time we saw Commander with a girl; they said he "changed horses." I saw the new girl was Mira. If she wasn't my first crush I'd have forgotten all this.' He chuckles.

'Who's Commander?'

'Led the Celestial Dragons. I forget his real name. Everyone called him Commander. Lived in the next building—number twelve.'

'Celestial Dragons?'

'I thought Jin Zhilong told you everything. There were two gangs in the twenty-four buildings—Commander's Celestial Dragons and Howitzer's Wild Fires. Commander was very popular then—he changed girlfriends like shirts. You remember that lunatic on the corner? They say he drove her crazy.'

'Really?'

'Her family said she went crazy because she failed the university entrance exams but I never believed it.'

'Me neither.'

'One night I came home after catching crickets and saw Commander and Mira slip out of the pillbox. I didn't know then what they were doing in there.' He giggles. 'Remember the pillbox?'

'Mira is my mother.' I hear my voice echo through the din.

He sets his glass down looking pleasantly surprised. 'I heard that way back I forget when but thought it was a joke.'

'No joke.'

'You don't look like her at all.'

'You mean I'm ugly?'

'I'm not a smooth talker. You're beautiful in a different way.'

'Maybe I look like my father.'

'Who's your father?'

'Who do you think?'

'How would I know?'

'You just said it.'

'Commander? No way—died too long ago.' He shakes his head.

'In the gang war the spring of 1976?'

'You didn't exist then.'

'I was in my mother's womb.'

Jianjun asks if I want a lift home. I say it is early—how about a drive around town? 'I never rode in a Lamborghini before.'

'How did you know I drive a Lamborghini?'

'I know a thing or two.'

We walk through the courtyard garden toward an underground parking garage. In contrast with summer no insects chirp, no glasses clink. Lamps are off. Gaunt trees line the pathway. Without Jianjun I would find it too spooky and sinister to continue.

He studies me and says, 'You really look like Commander.'

'What did he look like?'

'Also tall and thin like a bamboo pole. You're not like a bamboo pole of course.'

'You really know how to sweet-talk.'

'Told you I'm awkward.'

'Did he have small eyes, too?'

'Don't recall. He was darker than you though. Your mother was fair.'

I take a deep breath of chilly air. 'I feel much better now.'

'Me too.'

'Knowing my father is dead doesn't make me sad—it's a relief.'

'Why be sad?'

'No reason.'

'Everything's fated. What will happen, must; what won't, can't. I'm not afraid of anything now. With the cricket book here to protect us nothing can go wrong.'

'You can't be that superstitious.'

'It's not superstition, it's fact.'

'The cricket book won't protect me.'

'Of course it will. You rescued it.'

We take the lift down to the parking level. A half minute later the door opens. Phosphorescent lamps overhead illuminate cars parked around the garage. A scarlet sports car gleams in the distance. I feel lucky I did not go straight home. Otherwise I would have missed hearing all Jianjun had to tell me. The answer I sought so long came so easy. I entertain his motto: 'Everything's fated.' The solution to the mystery reveals itself in due time. The torment I endured the last few weeks tested my resolve to know. As long as I dare face adversity a way ahead will open up.

'What time is your flight tomorrow?'

'Eight.'

'So early? Too bad we can't drive around town all night.'

'It's dangerous for a girl to be out all night.'

'I'm not afraid.'

'You're strange.'

He takes car keys from his pants pocket. The Lamborghini shines a meter ahead of us.

'OK, I'll drive you around all you like.'

Someone jumps up from behind the Lamborghini. Jianjun screams and drops to the floor, his sunglasses skipping away.

'Fuck!' he shouts, his left hand clasping his lower back above the hip, blood streaming through his fingers.

Behind him stands a matron staring blankly. A bloody kitchen knife falls from her hand and clatters on the ground.

Jianjun reaches for the knife. She awakes as from a trance when the knife strikes her Achilles tendon and she falls.

I want to lift Jianjun up but on second thought leap over him and fling the knife away. I grab my cell phone and dial 112 but get a recorded message: 'Hello. For police please dial 110. For fire department please dial 119. For medical emergency please dial 120. For traffic incidents please dial 122 …' I dial 120 but get no signal. I try 110—ditto.

I run to the lift, take it to ground level, and dial 120 again.

'How may I help you?'

'Ambulance—we need an ambulance.'

'What are the symptoms please?'

'Someone's been stabbed and is losing blood fast.'

'Address please.'

'South Ocean Hotel, underground parking garage.'

'May I have the patient's name and age?'

'Yu Jianjun, about forty.'

'May I have your name and phone number?'

'Yang Lan, 15855769321.'

'An ambulance is on its way. Please stay where you are, don't leave the scene.'

I hang up and start to dial 110 but decide to check on Jianjun first. I run back to the lift and press the down button. It lights up red, hurting my eyes in the dark. I hear the lift engage and rise up toward me. The noise stops, the door opens slowly. The lift descends slowly too—stairs would be quicker if there were any.

Back in the parking garage I see the woman has disappeared. Drops of blood make a dotted line to the exit ramp. Jianjun lies beside the Lamborghini in a widening pool of blood—his face pale, his good eye barely open, his bad eye yellow-gray with white speckles on the cornea.

'The ambulance will be here soon.' I kneel beside Jianjun unsure whether to lift him.

'Glasses.' He gestures with one hand toward the sunglasses a meter away.

I pick them up, wipe the blood off with a Kleenex, and put them back on him. He smiles faintly.

Taking off my shawl, I fold and press it against the wound to stem the bleeding. How can there be so much blood? I stare into his face—it is turning purple. I avert my eyes and look at the vehicle entrance.

My palm gets damp. I turn the shawl over and press the clean side against the wound. My fingers get sticky, I smell rust. Where is the ambulance?

Hearing a siren I press the shawl down harder, release it, and stand up to signal the ambulance. Dizziness seizes me—I lean against a concrete pillar and close my eyes.

When I open them, everything is red: red car, red people, red shoes, red hands, red glasses, red floor, red ceiling, red air … I feel like I did standing in the winter sun thirty years ago. My nanny tells me to close my eyes and say what I see. I say red. She says it is the color of the sun and blood.

Revelation

26

It is bright outside when I wake up in my old bed at my aunt's and feel a headache throb. My aunt says I fainted and hit my head against a pillar. I touch my head and feel a gauze bandage as big as my hand.

She takes me to the hospital the next day. The doctor grants two weeks' sick leave saying concussion needs rest: come back in two weeks for a checkup and if need be, take extra sick leave. Brother Jin phones my aunt's and says not to worry—I can return to work whenever I feel up to it.

My aunt and uncle take sedulous care of me. They forbid reading books and newspapers or fetching my laptop and limit the time I can watch TV. Lest I get bored my aunt chats all day long, gossiping about this or that family, past or present, but avoids one topic—my birth. I do not want to think about it either, fearing morbid thoughts will irrupt if I open my mind. But Ray slips back in when I let down my guard. He has not called since he left. I do not know if he got over jet leg, started his new job, or misses me. Several times I think to call Linda and ask after him but when I pick up the phone I lose the mood.

Bored, I usurp my aunt's household chores. She shouts as if I break a taboo: 'Lie down and rest!'

'Stay home all day doing nothing and I'll get loony like Lulu.'

'Shut up with that nonsense!' My joke does not amuse her.

I laugh, push her down on the couch, and go to the kitchen.

I am at my aunt and uncle's a week when Jianhua and Brother Jin turn up with bags of medicinal food.

'Sorry to visit so late,' Jianhua says, walking into the living room.

'Sorry you had to come all this way.'

'How do you feel?'

'Not bad.'

'You look well.'

'The doctor says it's no big deal—I'll soon recover fully.'

'Don't be frivolous. Any little thing can do serious damage. You need rest and no stress.'

She looks worn out. Her crow's-feet are much deeper—she became a matron overnight.

'How's Jianjun?'

'Still in hospital, nothing too serious. The muscle is damaged—needs time to heal—but the kidney's all right.'

She pulls me to sit with her on the couch and lays her hand on top of mine. 'Lan we're so sorry. Jianjun got what he deserves; you didn't.'

'That's not your fault.'

'We still have to make amends. Jianjun too.'

'No matter as long as everyone's OK.'

'What's all this about?' my aunt intrudes.

'A gambler's wife from Wuhan tried to kill Jianjun with a kitchen knife. Her husband lost all they had.'

'Heavens! What did they gamble on?'

'Crickets, what else?'

'Gambling is China's ancestral sin,' my uncle remarks.

'Crickets ruined our family.' Jianhua's eyes redden.

Brother Jin hands her a Kleenex. 'It's lunchtime,' he says.

'Let's go out and get something simple.'

My aunt concurs.

Outside for the first time in a week I find the air makes me giddy. Her high heels clacking on the sidewalk, Jianhua asks me something now and then; I answer vaguely. In radiant sunshine the cold wind abrades. I close my eyes and see red—undulating blood. I open them at once and feel my heart pound—I want to throw up. Jianhua and Brother Jin catch me and ask if I am all right. 'Fine,' I hear myself whisper.

We arrive at a local chain restaurant. It is full. We have to wait fifteen minutes before getting seated. Our table is in the middle of a cacophonous dining hall. Annoyed, Jianhua summons a waitress and asks for a private dining room. The waitress says it requires a reservation.

'Not for a lunch party,' Jianhua retorts.

'It does here.'

'Why here and nowhere else? Look, it's empty.' Jianhua points to a private dining room. 'Is this a business or what? Who's your manager?'

'That room is reserved.'

'Who's your manager?'

'Drop it,' Brother Jin says. 'This table will do.'

'It's fine here,' my aunt adds.

Jianhua nags the waitress another five minutes before calming down. The waitress walks off fuming. We glance at each other, saying nothing.

'How's Wizard?' my aunt then asks Jianhua.

'He's all right, just worried about Jianjun.'

'You said he'll be OK, didn't you?'

Jianhua sighs: 'When he got to the hospital the police put him under guard. They found a heroin cache at his dog-racing track down south. As soon as he's well he goes on trial.'

My aunt frowns.

'The police are investigating. Jianjun says he's innocent—someone stashed it there to frame him. When his people heard he was under police guard they all said they knew nothing.'

My aunt shakes her head. 'People are like that.'

'A good lawyer can get him off,' my uncle says.

'That's best,' Jianhua replies, 'but finding one isn't easy. Dad says they should lock him up for good.'

'He's just saying that—he's really worried,' my aunt says.

'Of course.' Jianhua turns to Brother Jin. 'Ask your friends if they know a good criminal lawyer.'

'I only know business lawyers.'

'Ask your friends if they know a good criminal lawyer!'

'There's a big difference between business and criminal lawyers.'

'Last time you said you didn't know one either but you found Judge Wu.'

'Last time was different. It was gambling—three-year stretch max. Cash under the table was enough. This time it's narcotics—get real.'

'That's why we need help fast!'

'Wait till they finish the investigation then let's see what we can do.'

'Are you helping or not?'

'Narcotics is different. Nobody wants to get involved. We've got to be careful.'

'It was you who took Jianjun to Master Liang. Without you Jianjun wouldn't be in all this trouble.'

'Blame me again …'

'Who's Master Liang?' my aunt asks.

'Someone Zhilong used to know who borrowed money to start a business. When Jianjun got out of jail twenty years ago and had to rejoin society, Zhilong took him to Master Liang.' She turns to her husband: 'You knew Master Liang was a cricket-gambling addict. You set Jianjun up with him; you knew it was bad from the start.'

'That was crickets, this is narcotics. Don't mix everything up.'

'It all comes back to crickets! Without them the Wuhan gambler's wife wouldn't come all the way here to kill Jianjun. He wouldn't attract the police or be in all this narcotics shit.'

'All right, all right,' my aunt tries to calm her.

But Jianhua cannot stop accusing her husband: 'You kicked the habit. So everything's fine? My brother and father don't have your smarts. All they know is crickets. I asked you to give Jianjun a job and teach him something useful but you found excuses not to. Now he's in real trouble—he could get years behind bars or even shot!' She sobs.

Brother Jin frowns silently. Everyone else keeps quiet too.

'Being too clever isn't good either,' my uncle breaks in.

'Fools can have good luck,' Jianhua says, and blows her nose. 'Nobody in my family is stupid but we all have bad luck. Who knows when I'll go down.'

'Jianhua, don't fret,' my aunt says. 'You're living a lady's life others pray for but can't have.'

'That's a good one! My daughter is a rotten student and my husband, you see, is a selfish high-lifer—he couldn't care less if his in-laws live or die.'

Brother Jin's face is steely; he says nothing.

'All right Jianhua,' my aunt says. 'We know you're worried

about Jianjun—we are too. But getting together like this isn't easy—don't spoil it.'

Brother Jin nudges his wife: 'Today we came to visit Lan. We can talk family business at home.'

Jianhua forces a smile. 'Lan, don't take me seriously; I'll shut up. Come on, eat, eat.'

The food looks good but tastes insipid. I do not know whether to blame the chef or our mood. Revenge of the waitress? We eat silently as if doing a chore.

Time to leave at last.

'I'm thinking this won't be over soon,' Jianhua tells me outside the restaurant. 'Why don't we take a little vacation to unwind? Ting just had midterms. You come along!'

'Go with them,' my aunt says before I can respond. 'Try to relax.'

27

A week later Jianhua, Ting, Brother Jin, Wizard, and I arrive at a resort hotel outside Yangshuo overlooking the Li River. The hotel is a renovated country estate house owned by a couple—local wife, Australian husband. The personnel are all girls about twenty with basic English and big smiles.

We plan to stay four days, Friday through Monday, so Ting will miss only two days of school. Flying to Guilin Thursday evening we meet the hotel manager, who for three hundred yuan drives us in from the airport an hour away. When we reach the hotel it is pitch-dark. Two red lanterns glow outside the driveway gate. In the lobby two foreigners sit at two public computers. The receptionist dozes with a teach-yourself-English book open on the desk in front of her. Wizard coughs. She wakes up apologetically, says our rooms are ready, and gets busy with registration paperwork.

The rooms are better than I expected—spacious, clean, and tasteful with antique décor. They have Wi-Fi but no phone or television. Jianhua and Brother Jin take one room, Wizard gets another, Ting and I share a third. Tired from the journey I shower, put on pajamas, and see Ting go online with her iPhone before I fall asleep soon after lying on the bed.

When I wake up the next morning fog shrouds the river. I step out on the balcony, inhale fresh air, and watch the morning sun dispel the mist. The jagged peaks across the river look as if painted on an unfurling scroll. I see Wizard doing tai chi on the terrace below. I hear Jianhua say she wants to exercise too and see her step out in a sporty outfit.

'Sleep well?' Brother Jin asks from the balcony next door.

'Just fine,' I answer, startled by his presence.

'Nice here isn't it?'

'Excellent feng shui.'

'Guess who chose it.'

'Who else?'

He smiles and stretches. 'I'll shower and check on breakfast.'

'What's our plan today?'

'Don't know; Jianhua is in charge.'

He slips back into the room.

I close my eyes against the rising sun and see no blood. I feel grateful to this family and do not know how life would be without them now—probably empty and dull. Barely four months passed since I came home but compared with ten uneventful years abroad, they seem like a lifetime. I wonder if it is all a dream I shall wake up from to discover nothing really happened. Maybe I am dreaming ten thousand meters up on the airplane flying home. My body feels buoyant.

'Lan, come down to breakfast!' Brother Jin's voice interrupts the reverie.

'Coming!'

I quickly change clothes and head for the door but stop to scribble a note to Ting, still asleep.

Jianhua has arranged for us to tour the Li River on a motorized bamboo raft. Ting wants to go kayaking and sulks when told she cannot. Jianhua has everything ready—bottled water, bread, snacks, sunblock, umbrella—because buying supplies on the trip would be difficult. About every kilometer along the way, however, is a pebble beach where peddlers sell them. At lunchtime we stop at one. Brother Jin disappears and returns a few minutes later with deep-fried fish and shrimp on spits. Ting discards the bread she was nibbling. Brother Jin and I dig in as well. Wizard has a taste and says it is too greasy. Jianhua declines, calling it unhygienic.

'These peaks look just like they do on postcards,' Jianhua says. 'Pity there's no mist—it would be romantic.'

'You can always spray a mouthful of water at the sky,' Brother Jin says with a laugh.

'Idiot.' Jianhua glares back. 'Li River water looks as clear as on the postcards too.'

'Not that clear,' Ting says stirring water with one hand.

'Don't get your hands dirty, you're still eating.'

'But you said the water is clear.'

'I said clear not clean.' Jianhua looks away, eyes raised. 'Are you crazy?'

I turn around and see Brother Jin—shoes, socks, shirt, and denims on the beach—step into the water in his boxer shorts. A thin stripe of dark hair runs up his flat abdomen.

'It's not cold. There're a lot of people swimming.'

'They're locals, they're used to it!'

Not bothering to talk back, Brother Jin dives into the river.

'Damn,' Jianhua says, 'I forgot to bring a towel.'

Ting and I take off our shoes, role up our pant legs, and step into the water. The pebbles beneath make our feet uncomfortable and we soon come ashore. Jianhua takes a sweatshirt from her carry bag so we can dry our feet but changes her mind, saying she will save it for Brother Jin to dry off with. The boatman tosses us an old cloth; we take turns drying our feet. When we put our socks and shoes on we see a shivering

Brother Jin dry himself with Jianhua's sweatshirt.

'I'm getting old, not like before.'

'Quick,' Jianhua says, 'get your clothes on. Don't gab.'

Brother Jin steps under the roof of the raft and, with only the sweatshirt for cover, adroitly slips out of his boxer shorts into his denims.

After a few minutes' more rest we again board the raft. Jianhua takes three preserved plums from her purse and offers one each to Ting and me, keeping one for herself. Ting declines—she is enchanted with a video camera, panning full circle around her.

'You're a good swimmer,' I tell Brother Jin.

'I learned from Chairman Mao.'

'Tell me what you can't do.'

'That's a tough one.'

'I didn't know you knew crickets—it's why you caught one so fast at Jade's party.'

'Catching crickets is easy.'

'The one you caught became Shanghai champion, you know?'

'Zhilong caught General Guan?' Wizard asks.

'To amuse Lan.'

'Catching a good bug is always like that—try hard you never catch one, by chance you catch a champion.'

'I'd never guess your husband was once into crickets,' I tell Jianhua.

'How could I be in her family and not into crickets?' Brother Jin says with a wry look at his wife.

'Shut up,' she replies. 'Don't mention crickets if you don't want a fight.'

'You were into crickets before you met us,' Wizard says.

'Shanghai guys all do crickets—when I came there I did too. That's a long time ago—almost forty years.'

'Did you fight crickets with Blind?' I ask.

'Blind?' Jianhua asks.

'The myopic kid in building fourteen who got killed,' Brother Jin says.

Ting holds the video camera up to his face. 'Don't fool around,' he says, pushing it away.

'Oh that little bastard,' Wizard says. 'Didn't he steal our cricket book?'

'What cricket book?' Jianhua asks.

'Your family talisman,' Brother Jin says.

'Oh, *that* book!'

'Lan, didn't you promise to look ahead not behind and never dig up old dirt?'

'I didn't dig up dirt. I just asked how you know crickets.'

'How did the cricket book wind up next door?' Wizard asks. 'Did Blind ever tell you?'

'Next door?' Brother Jin asks.

'My aunt and uncle's old apartment,' I say. 'I guess I never told you but my uncle found it in my cousin's room and sold it to a secondhand bookshop.'

'Oh?'

'Blind gave it to Commander who had my mother hide it. She hid it at my aunt's. Blind and Commander got killed, she died, and Wizard thought Blind's gang burned it.' I ignored all this for weeks but the data I gathered fit together as a story.

'Did you make all that nonsense up?' Jianhua asks.

'Jianjun told me.'

'How could he know?'

'He told me some things; the rest I figured out.'

'I'm totally confused.'

'There's something more complicated—about my parents.'

'You know who your father is?' Brother Jin asks.

'Commander.'

'Blind's gang leader?'

'You knew him too?'

'Only by name.'

'Who's that?' Jianhua asks.

'My father.'

'Jianjun told you that?'

'He said Commander was my mother's boyfriend so he must be the one.'

'You believe Jianjun?'

'What else did he tell you?' Wizard interrupts.

'Not much—just stuff about the past. He's got a good memory.'

'What could he know?' Jianhua says. 'How old was he then? Even I don't remember.'

'You've got a selective memory.' Brother Jin says. 'You remember only what you want to and forget the rest.'

'I don't remember as much as you—that's for sure. Why remember old crap from the past? Why grow gray hair for nothing?' She runs her fingers through his hair above one ear. 'Look at your gray hair.'

'What was Commander's real name?' I ask Brother Jin.

'I don't know. Everybody called him Commander.'

'Which kid do you mean?' Wizard asks.

'Jianjun said he lived in number twelve,' I say.

'Twelve? That must be Old Shi's kid.'

'Old Shi?'

'I knew him well,' he says proudly. 'We came back from Korea together and went to work at the factory about the same time. I knew his wife too and watched their two boys grow up. Completely different, those two. The oldest was always the best and brightest. The youngest was always fooling around and making trouble for the family. Old Shi and his wife worried about him all the time but couldn't control him so it all went bad.'

'You mean the troublemaker was my father?'

'Your parents are your aunt and uncle,' Wizard says sternly. 'They raised you and saw to your education. Understand gratitude and reciprocity.'

'Understood.'

Jianhua has us on a tight schedule. After dinner in Yangshuo we watch an open-air folk dance. The next day we go by boat to see a thousand-year-old town, an ethnic minority village, several temples, and some caves. The third day we hire a minivan to visit a national park. We return to the hotel at evening and have dinner in the restaurant. Jianhua wants to go souvenir shopping in Yangshuo and Ting wants to go barhopping. Brother Jin says he will escort Ting: 'Let your mother shop by herself—I'd rather drink beer.' He asks whether I will join them or Jianhua. I say I will keep Wizard company and turn in early.

After they leave Wizard and I order a pot of green tea.

'Does the Shi family still live in the twenty-four buildings?'

'They left a long time ago. Shi and his wife went to babysit their grandchildren in America ten years ago. Their son got a PhD there and married late. The kids are mixed-blood twins. His wife is white American.'

'Are you still in touch?'

'No, they don't come back anymore—no relatives here. I hear there're a lot of Chinese in LA so life should be comfortable.'

‘LA?’

‘So I recall. I don’t know America—the only places I heard of are New York and LA.’

I miss Ray. I should visit him and look up my grandparents and the uncle I never knew.

Back in my room I sit up in bed. Wind through a half-open window brings the southern chill in. I imagine knocking at the door of a suburban home outside LA. The door opens; my grandparents answer; sunlight shines on their faces. They invite me in, show me photos of my father, and tell me stories of his childhood.

Now the tangled stories from my parents’ generation unravel. I am surprised at the simplicity of it all: teenage boy meets teenage girl; they eat forbidden fruit and beget me by accident; the cricket book is proof of their affair. I can see my mother’s youthful face clearly; my father transforms from an abstract notion into a distinct image—he is tall, slender, dark, and taut; his slant eyes and thin lips are not handsome but charming.

My parents would have met on a summer afternoon when the gentle screech of cicadas filled the sultry air. Did they fall in love at once or did they first admire each other from a distance? They rendezvoused by the river and made love in the pillbox in front of their building. One clear winter night I was conceived.

They were as unaware of my existence as they were of being stalked by Loony Lulu, who loved my father and dreamed of being his girl. Jealousy consumed her; she had hallucinations …

As for the cricket book, Blind was the culprit. Jianguo could not bear his parents’ anguish at losing their prize heirloom and persuaded Howitzer, the rival gang leader, to get it back.

When Blind learned Howitzer was after the book he got my father to have my mother hide it. She had no inkling what it meant and forgot she hid it at my aunt's.

The cricket book started a feud between the two gangs in the twenty-four buildings. The grievance was forgotten but the feud escalated anyway. The showdown came one spring midnight on the bright-yellow rape plant field across the river. Spilt blood shone like dark water in the moonlight. A large crowd gathered after sunrise. Wailing echoed for hours on end.

People in the twenty-four buildings quit feeling miserable only that fall, the next cricket season. Word that the Yang family adopted a baby girl revived their glib optimism. Rumor had it she was a foundling—blind, deaf, crippled, hermaphroditic, or incestuous. But Loony Lulu's fantasy fit the facts—the girl was Commander and Mira's love child.

Why did my mother carry me to term? Pity for the unborn, esteem for my father killed in the midnight battle, or failure to abort in time? All I can guess is that the baby girl gave people in the twenty-four buildings something to gossip about; when they gossiped about her, irrepressible joy beamed from their faces as if all cruelty and helplessness vanished then and there.

28

Coming home from Yangshuo I feel energized—these four days away were physically tiring but I slept well.

'I'll go back to work tomorrow,' I tell Brother Jin.

'What's the hurry?'

'I'm fully recovered.'

'If you feel up to it go ahead. Your call.'

Back at my aunt and uncle's that evening I rummage through my clothes but find nothing I can wear to work.

'I'll go fetch clothes from my place,' I tell my aunt.

'Don't hurry back to work. Take another day or two off to get healthy again. It won't matter to the company.'

'If I stay home too long I'll get loony like Lulu.'

Magic name—she shuts up at once.

I check the time. Almost nine. 'OK it's too late. I won't go in tomorrow.'

'Get checked at the hospital. If you're OK go to work the day after.'

I do not object.

The checkup results in a clean bill of health. The doctor says to resume work anytime but not use a computer more than two hours at a stretch. I relax about clothes and dress casually for the office.

Not told I would return, my colleagues are surprised to see me the next day. They walk up and ask: *Are you feeling better?*

What was the matter with you? Do you need more rest? Their solicitude betrays pleasure at another's misfortune.

At noon Amy invites me to lunch. When no one is within earshot she whispers, 'The whole office says you lost your mind.'

'Do I look crazy?'

'Must be that bitch Nancy spreading the rumor.'

'I hit my head.'

'How?'

'Hit a pillar—I fainted at the sight of blood.'

'You donated blood?'

'No, I witnessed an incident.'

'Traffic accident?'

'No, a stabbing.'

'You scare me!'

But seeing nothing wrong, she changes the subject: 'Little Boss left.'

'He said he'd leave after New Year's.'

'Big Boss said he got a good offer and chose to take it.'

'So fast! Big Boss didn't tell me anything.'

'Tell you a secret—don't tell anyone: Big Boss kicked him out. Someone overheard them fight. Big Boss wanted to pay a bribe to get an overseas contract. Little Boss was afraid of getting caught so Big Boss kicked him out. He even had the board fire him officially for leaking company secrets. Don't tell anyone!'

'I won't,' I say but recall Little Boss impugning honesty at the top.

'Promise! If Big Boss ever finds out our heads will roll.'

'Trust me not to squeal. Who'll replace Little Boss?'

'They're going to announce a vacancy soon but we think

Big Boss already has someone in mind. He won't take a stranger.' She giggles. 'Nancy already recommended herself. While you were out the old slut hung around Big Boss everyday in a miniskirt. Playing Lolita at her age—so disgusting! If she gets the job I'll die on the spot in front of everybody.'

'No way. Big Boss isn't stupid.'

'Why don't you apply?'

'Me? Get out!'

'Maybe you're the one he has in mind.'

'I wouldn't take the job if he asked me. Managing people is too big a hassle.'

'Such a great opportunity—you can't throw it away, especially to Nancy!'

'You're a kinky fantasist.'

'Don't forget to make me your personal assistant in the back office.'

'Not going to happen, forget it.'

After work Amy invites me out shopping. She skips dinner—says she is on a diet. I get a hamburger at McDonald's and eat as we walk. We finish shopping at ten-thirty. My shopping bags bulge with a skirt, two pairs of jeans, a hat, and a pair of boots. I contemplate buying a winter coat but think it too expensive. Amy buys nothing and will wait for the Christmas sale. I tell her I have to buy what I like when I see it or it will be gone the next time I come round. She says I am a rich girl who does not understand a poor girl's hardship.

After saying goodnight I go straight to my apartment. The mailbox in the hallway is crammed. Newspapers lie on the floor. Too tired to tidy up I open the door. Everything is covered with three weeks of dust. A stale but cozy smell fills the air. I find forty-eight unread emails in my laptop. Most are junk, which I zap. I check the rest one by one. Nothing from Ray.

Being home without Ray feels strange. Part of my soul is gone and I have no idea how to fix it. There is a T-shirt on the bed he forgot to pack. I bury my face in it but cannot smell him. I fold it up, put it in the closet, and vacuum the apartment. Then I change the bedclothes and pillowcases.

Loneliness consumes me.

I forget who said one has to face loneliness eventually. For the first time in my life I feel like getting married. Is it too late to reconnect with Ray? I write him an email to ask how he is doing but say nothing about myself.

The company is busier than ever as year-end approaches. Brother Jin is off to America, goes to Europe from there, and comes back just before Christmas. The office is chaotic with Little Boss gone. With no authority over them, colleagues goof off at every opportunity. I have no opportunity—old work needs doing as new work pours in. I never go home before nine and Christmas comes and goes before I know it.

After five New Year's Eve colleagues knock off one by one.

Amy walks up: 'Any plans for tonight?'

'No, nothing. I didn't realize it was New Year's Eve till late this morning.'

'I'm going with my boyfriend to Xintiandi for the countdown. Want to come along?'

'I don't want to chaperone.'

'No way, come join us.'

'Knock yourselves out. Holidays aren't for me. Any day is good enough to celebrate if you're in the mood.'

'I'm not on your case. Call if you change your mind.' She throws a kiss.

Soon the office is empty. After six I am the only one left staring at a computer screen. Now I too want to go out for some fun: staying home alone on a global party night is too sad. Seeing the director's office light still on, I email Brother Jin: 'Quit work—tell Jianhua and Ting to come out and party.'

A few seconds later he replies: 'Let me call home.'

I hear him talking on the phone. The talking soon stops. He walks out of his office toward me.

'Jianhua has a date with her masseur. Ting is out with friends. I'm the only one left.'

'Where shall we go?'

'I'm in the middle of something—give me half an hour. Think where you want to go.'

I wait till seven-thirty when he finally quits work.

'Sorry I'm late.'

'I have no plans tonight anyway.'

'Know where you want to go?'

'I'm starving. Let's have dinner.'

'What's your pleasure?'

'Whatever satisfies.'

'You're easy to please. Let's go someplace good.'

We catch a taxi. It stops three minutes later at a French restaurant in a renovated church with a dome.

'So close? We could've walked.'

'You said you were starving—I thought you couldn't wait.'

I poke his arm with my fist.

New Year's decorations on the front door cover unremoved Christmas decorations. The dome inside sports a fake renaissance fresco. Beneath it stands a young woman in an evening gown playing the violin. A waiter in black tuxedo asks if we have a reservation. Brother Jin says no.

'I'm sorry, we're full.'

'Got here too late,' Brother Jin says apologetically.

'No big deal. Let's go someplace else.'

In summer this part of town is a labyrinth of little streets lined by shade trees. Now it is winter and the tree trunks look like thick bare thighs. There are many restaurants to choose from. Shaded by lush trees in summer they are subdued and inviting. Tonight they are raucous and obtrusive. We chat while walking. Whenever we see a place that looks attractive we walk in, but everything is full.

'Why did Jason leave so suddenly?'

'I wanted him to stay longer but he said he had to go.'

'What went wrong?'

'He violated business ethics.'

'Jason? I can't imagine.'

'I didn't see it coming either but when it did I had to …'

'What did he do?'

'None of your business.'

'Who'll replace him?'

'Are you interested?'

'Me?'

'Don't be shy. You'd be good at it. I need someone I can trust.'

'May I have a few days to think it over?'

'Let me know at work the day after tomorrow. No time to lose.'

'OK.'

'How've you been?'

'Not bad just busy. Any news of Jianjun?'

'Medical or legal?'

'Both.'

'Medical OK, legal rough.'

'Any chance he'll get off?'

‘It seems I’m the one who has to think how.’

‘Well?’

‘It will cost a lot of money but money is not magic.’

‘You try hard to help but he seems ungrateful.’

‘That’s him all over.’

‘Seems he hates you.’

‘Always did.’

‘He blames you for his eye.’

‘Told you that too? No idea why he believes that shit.’

‘Called you a wily old fox.’

‘Whether that’s an insult depends on what’s meant by wily.’

‘What do you mean by it?’

‘Any businessman’s wily. In business you’ve got to cope with circumstances—fast. It doesn’t mean you’ve got to cheat. Jianjun’s been chiseling forever but can’t protect himself in a crunch. That’s not wily, it’s stupid.’

‘Slippery not cunning.’

‘Precisely. Like Blind that way—boastful for fear of being looked down on. Got a lot of shady friends—even criminals who did time. No wonder he ends up a fall guy. So guilty by association that a river couldn’t wash the filth away.’

‘Blind was a fall guy too?’

‘I mean they had the same weakness. Both craved attention and got it through fighting. But whether you win or lose a fight you suffer. The real winner is whoever profits.’

‘Clam grabs heron’s beak and fisherman catches both.’

‘Exactly. That I learned from the gang war at the twenty-four-buildings. Ever since I told myself to keep a low profile—watch but don’t get involved unless you have to.’

‘Mustn’t be easy for someone like you.’

‘No, I’m still learning.’

'Who was the fisherman in the gang war?'

'Whoever got the cricket book.'

'It wound up with my cousin—hardly a fisherman.'

'Forget what I said.'

'If Commander's gang was the clam and Howitzer's was the heron, who was the fisherman?'

'Maybe nobody.'

'Too bad all the witnesses are dead and there's no evidence left.'

'It's all right—may the living enjoy peace and quiet. What did Jianjun tell you exactly?'

'Blind stole the cricket book, my parents fell in love, Lulu went crazy. You know where I was conceived?'

'Where?'

'In the pillbox! I felt drawn to it as a child—I found it cozy inside like home. Weird, huh?'

A motor scooter darts past from behind. He pulls me closer.

'They did it in the pillbox?'

'Apparently.'

'Impossible.'

'Why?'

'Too cramped.'

'Where else could they do it?'

'By the river, in the farm fields—lots of places.'

'You know your way around.'

He laughs and slips his arm around me; his hand rests on my hip. My skin tingles warmly beneath winter clothes.

'You were right to tell me not to talk to Loony Lulu. If I had obeyed she would still be at her window daydreaming about Commander.'

He removes his hand. 'What?'

'The night after I talked to her she went out to meet him and drowned in a creek.'

'She's dead?'

'So sad—wasted her life on fantasy love.'

'How do you know?'

'I went by and saw her mother crying—neighbors told me.'

'I thought Jianjun …'

'Jianjun only said Loony Lulu was crazy about Commander and lost her mind when he got involved with my mother.'

'Couldn't happen.'

'No?'

'Lulu had no contact with Commander—they never spoke.'

'How do you know?'

'I knew Lulu sane.'

'Call her Loony Lulu like everyone else. Call her Lulu and it sounds like you had something going with her.'

'I did.'

'What?'

'What do you think?'

'You and she …'

He looks me straight in the eye. 'I was at the worker-peasant-soldier university. She was in high school—fifteen or sixteen, pretty and smart.' He looks away.

'Why are you so sure she never knew Commander?'

'I know she didn't like him—too hoody for her.'

'Then what drove her crazy?'

He says nothing. In the streetlamp light I see his cheek tremble. 'Tonight I trust you with a secret,' he says. 'I never believed failing the university entrance exams drove her crazy though everyone said so—I thought it was my fault, but I never made sure because I didn't want trouble.'

‘What did you do to her?’

‘I was young and impulsive. She and I had squabbles but nothing bad enough to drive anyone crazy.’ He rubs his face with both hands. ‘That spring I was sent away for a spell. When I got back I heard there’d been a gang war and she was with relatives downtown. I went by her home every few days—I was worried and wanted to get something I left with her. But her parents slammed the door in my face. I guessed they found us out. Our affair was underground: students weren’t allowed to date and—worse—I was head of the department’s Party branch.’

‘Communist Party?’

‘What else?’

‘How could the Party admit a sly fox like you?’

‘Why not? I’m so small.’

‘You? Small?’

‘Compared to the organization you’re always small. But you can ride it like a bus toward your own destination.’

‘Like what? Find Lulu?’

‘No, I didn’t wish to expose private matters.’

‘Then what did you do?’

‘Nothing I could do. The next time I saw her was a year later when she was already insane. I still don’t know what happened the month I was away. Visiting Wizard’s the last thirty years I always made a detour—I couldn’t stand seeing her. Jianhua teased me for avoiding that lunatic like a leper.’

‘Maybe the gang war pushed her over the edge,’ I say taking his hand, knowing no better way to show sympathy. ‘Maybe when you were away some other guy forced her.’ I implicate Commander but cannot believe my own father did that.

‘I thought that too. But what’s the point?’ He squeezes my

hand, releases it, slips his arm around my waist, and pulls me close to him.

'Why didn't you say you knew Lulu? When I mentioned her last time you lost your temper.'

'I did?'

'Really frightening.'

'Sorry about that.'

'Forget it. It's old dirt as you say—no need to dig it up.'

Our office building looms across the street.

'We made a lap,' he says. 'I have to take you to a good place tonight no matter how late it gets.'

'I don't care really—fast food, takeout, anything will do.'

'Do as I say or else I'll feel guilty.' He withdraws his arm and studies his Ulysse Nardin. 'Almost nine. I forgot something important—I've got to call Malta before they quit today.'

'When did we start doing business in Malta?'

'Malta's a very small place but may become our biggest project in Europe.'

'What project?'

'Shipping.'

'We do shipping now too?'

'I'll explain another time—after New Year's.'

He awaits an opportunity to cross the street.

'I'll come along.'

'Of course.'

On second thought I say, 'I'll get takeout on the way home and wait for you there.'

'Takeout's not good enough tonight.'

'Is if you know where to get it. You've been to my place. Remember?'

'I'll find it.'

'Call if you get lost.'

'I'll be quick.' He pats me on the shoulder and darts across the street.

I walk home. My hungry stomach no longer craves dinner; my heart swells bittersweet. I stop at the little restaurant near my apartment, skim the menu, and order pork chops, spicy shrimp, stir-fried Chinese broccoli, vegetable and meatball soup, steamed rice, and two bottles of beer. While I wait the owner asks why she has not seen me lately and where my handsome foreign guy is. In no mood to explain I evade her questions and leave as soon as the food appears.

In front of Joffre New Village I hear loud noise from Red Regime. A big poster on the wall says: WILD NEW YEAR'S EVE! WORLD-CLASS DJ! COUNTDOWN PARTY! FIREWORKS DISPLAY! ROCK TOGETHER! I think to watch the fireworks from my backyard with Brother Jin.

When I get home Brother Jin is not there. I unpack the takeout on the living room table and fetch two glasses, a stack of plates, two bowls, and chopsticks. The apartment is chilly like an igloo. I set the air conditioning on warm and fetch today's newspaper from the mailbox.

An envelope slips out. The handwriting on it is in English—must be from Ray! I take it to the living room but see Dutch stamps. I open it, see a letter, and find a smaller envelope inside it. I put the letter aside and study the small envelope—addressed to me in Holland ten years ago. The back is covered with Chinese stamps. I read the letter:

I kept this ten years and hope I did not cause you any trouble. I own the house that includes the apartment you used to live in. My husband and I bought it soon after you moved out. Then we got this letter addressed to you. I wrote 'addressee unknown' on it and left it outside the mailbox, but the post office redelivered it a few days later. No one I asked knew your new address. I put the letter away; many years passed. Two months ago my children found it and thought the stamps were very pretty. They opened it and showed me three pages with Chinese writing on them. Maybe it is important but I do not know, I cannot read it. I decided to look for you and found the bank you worked for here. They said you went back to China. Someone had your current address.

Again, I am sorry the envelope was opened. But you know how children are. If the letter contains anything sensitive do not worry: no one who saw it here can read it. I should have found you earlier and hope it is not important.

Friendly greetings, Euphra van Gom

Who wrote me ten years ago? The small envelope is sealed with Scotch tape; I open it and take out the letter. I recognize my late cousin's handwriting:

Lan, I hope this letter finds you well. We are all fine. Your aunt and uncle are in good health and I have new plans. Lan, you may not know it but I envied you all along. This may sound strange: Why would anyone envy a cousin fifteen years younger? But you will understand without my having to explain—I have nothing and cannot live a normal life, you have everything I desire on earth. You are pretty and smart; you are surrounded by people who love and care for you; you have great prospects. You always say you have no parents but that is no excuse for self-pity. We all love you.

To be honest, your going abroad really hurt me. But having decided to write this letter there is nothing I feel too ashamed of to confess to you. I hated you lately—not because of anything you did to hurt me but because you succeeded in going far away. You have no idea how I long to leave the twenty-four buildings and see the outside world. But I cannot. I have been teaching myself English in hopes of making a mental tour of the world through books. But the freer I feel mentally the more imprisoned I feel physically. I envy your making real what I could only dream of but never attain. Because you got it easily you may not treasure it enough. To me that is a crime.

But now I have thought it through: If I am stuck here why not bless someone dear to me when she gets the chance to get away? I watched you join our family and grow up—how can I not feel deeply for you? This you cannot doubt. What I want to say is: go away as far as you can and never come back. Your home is too dark, perverted, backward, cruel, and hypocritical. Go live in the civilized world and make a brand-new life for yourself. Your aunt and uncle will miss you so call them regularly and come back often to visit.

As for me, I have plans for the future. 'If you try you may fail but if you never try you cannot succeed,' a great mind says. I will forget my worries and go out into the world. I have no money or skills and moving about is hard for me. Maybe I will get lost or starve to death on the way but I am not afraid. Anything is better than wasting away in the twenty-four buildings.

I am almost forty. Any youth I might have had is gone. I am an old maid to be honest, but that does not mean I do not understand love. I love with my heart—that is enough. Yet I dream of meeting my better half on the journey. He may not be handsome; he may be disabled like me; but he must be a knowing man with compassion. I will follow him to the ends of the earth and stand by him no matter how hard life gets.

I withdrew all my savings from the bank—seventy-eight hundred yuan in total. I bought a one-way train ticket to Tibet. The rest of my money I can spend as I need to. I do not know if I will come back. Maybe I will when my money is gone. Maybe I will never come back. Promise never to tell your aunt and uncle! I love them more than anyone but their love stifles me. I have lived without air for almost forty years now and have to take a deep breath. If they ask, say I am fine and tell them not to worry but never say where I am. If they know they will certainly come looking for me. Remember, this is a secret between you and me.

Someone knocks. I put down the letter and answer the door.

Brother Jin holds up a bottle of red wine with one hand and, from behind his back, presents a bottle of champagne with the other.

'I already bought beer.'

'Beer? It's New Year's Eve! Open the wine now and chill the champagne in the fridge till midnight,' he says walking in.

I take the bottles and do as told.

'Who sent this?' he asks looking down at the letter as I appear with the open bottle in one hand and two wine glasses in the other.

'My cousin.'

'The one who went missing?'

'She sent it ten years ago; I got it just now.'

'Efficient post.'

'Check this.' I show him the cover letter; he hands it back. 'What happened?'

'She wrote it soon after I went abroad and sent it to a Dutch address I'd just moved away from.' I sit at the table; he sits opposite. 'The new landlady kept it ten years and traced me here the other day.'

'Why did she take ten years to trace you?'

'She meant well—it took her a lot of trouble to find me.'

'Good the letter finally reached you.'

'Hearing from my cousin after so long is a miracle like what happened with the cricket book.'

'Just looking at that book made you feel it was uncanny.'

'I thought you said you never saw it.'

'I meant Wizard never showed it to me. Come on, taste the wine. Don't talk all evening.'

He pours me a glass. I take a sip. 'I'm no good at this—taste it yourself.'

He rolls a sip of wine around in his mouth, swallows, and says, 'Not bad. It'll ripen when it gets some air.'

I put the letter on the couch, transfer the takeout food to plates, and hand him a bowl and chopsticks.

'Reading my cousin's letter feels weird.'

'She said something weird?'

'I'm not done reading it but she said she wanted to realize her dream and would run away to Tibet. Too bad she only wrote me one letter. Whatever happened to her probably happened soon after she left.'

He takes a bite of dinner. 'Separation and reunion like life and death are the way of the world: you've never lived through catastrophe—if you had you'd know there're things you must let go in order to continue.'

'My cousin is not the worst of it. She at least tried to get away. No matter what happened I'm proud of her. But Lulu's life was a total waste.'

'Insanity and idiocy are the way of the world too.' He puts down his chopsticks and looks at me. 'Promise me something.'

'What?'

'Don't talk about bad things tonight.'

I nod, sipping wine, which makes me warm.

'You chose good food,' he says after sampling each plate.

'I'm a regular there. The owner is nosy but serves good food.'

'Give me the address.'

'Remind me after dinner.' I get up. 'You brought red wine; I should light candles.'

'As you like.'

I check several cabinets but find no candles.

'Maybe Ray used them up at his party.' I sit back down at the table.

'How's he doing?'

'No word since he left.'

'You didn't call or write either?'

'No reply to my email so I let it go.'

'You guys are fast. I take you to Jade's and before I know it you're shacked up.'

'It's history I'm afraid.'

He says nothing.

'I guess he's right.'

'About what?'

'Love doesn't work long distance—it's shack up or break up.'

'True.'

'Dinner's getting cold; I'm a bad hostess.'

'You treat me like a guest.'

'Aren't you?'

His eyes jab like ice picks. I look down and take a few mouthfuls of rice.

'Shall I reheat dinner?'

'No.'

I stand up to clear the table. 'If we get hungry we can always go out. There'll be something open.'

'Always is.'

I put leftover dinner in the fridge. When I return to the table my glass is full.

'Don't give me so much, I'm not a big drinker.'

'Don't quit on me now. Anyway red wine is good for you. We've got to open the champagne soon.'

'Does Jianhua know you're here?'

'I told her there's an office party—I'm not due home till next year.' He stands up, steps round the table, puts his hands on my shoulders, and smells my hair.

'This isn't the office.'

'I'm with an office colleague—you're a witness.'

I cannot suppress a smile but say nothing.

'We can talk more comfortably on the couch.' He lifts me gently by the elbows and escorts me there asking, 'Did you invite me here with an ulterior motive?' His hand wanders.

'No.'

'Sorry.' He withdraws his hand. 'I misunderstood.'

He moves to get up.

I touch his wrist. He kisses me fully and forcefully on the mouth—so forcefully I almost fall over. He pulls me tight against him. I smell a faint mix of wine, dinner, cologne, and sweat. Oddly familiar signs of new intimacy.

My mind races: What am I doing? Do I really know him? What am I getting into?

I feel a slight abrasion above my upper lip.

Will Jianhua find out? Probably not. She would not want to know in any case and may well be in bed with her masseur right now.

His kiss softens.

'Bed?'

My unheated bedroom is ten degrees colder than the living room and the light is off. But the moon and the living room lamp illuminate the way. The bed is unmade, the quilt is rumpled—no time to tidy up this morning.

'Cold,' I say as we approach the bed.

'We'll warm each other up.'

The sheet and quilt are cold; his skin is warm. The air conditioning unit on the living room wall starts up, noisy as a fridge. I hear our breaths quicken. 'The way to a woman's heart,' Eileen Chang says somewhere, 'is through her vagina.' Sex fulfills, the heart fills. He feels heavy on top of me—I find it hard to breathe and gently push him off. He rolls over and lifts me on top so I ride him facing away.

He proceeds. Does he lead or follow? I cannot tell. It feels as if we rehearsed many times. Our reflection in the wardrobe mirror is ghostly.

We lie on our sides. He cuddles from behind, his forearm on my hip, his hand fondling my tummy. He is not asleep—I am not alone.

His cell phone rings.

Jianhua? I remove his hand.

Two seconds later he sits up, gets off the bed, and grabs his pants. Cold blue light flickers.

'Hello? … What can't wait till we're back at work here?'

Not Jianhua. He sits on the edge of the bed, phone clenched between ear and shoulder, pulling his pants up.

'Again? … Why didn't you say so earlier? Who's available this hour? … What are you waiting for? Just say it!'

He buckles his belt, throws his shirt over his shoulders, and walks to the living room.

I get up, dress, and go into the bathroom. The face in the mirror reflects afterglow. I brush my teeth, wash my face, and comb my hair. He shouts about 'the books' and 'a big hole.'

I enter the living room and see him at the window, facing outside, one hand holding the phone, the other resting on the windowsill. I pour myself another glass of wine and sit on the couch to read my cousin's letter—crumpled from his sitting on it.

There is another secret I kept from you all this time. You always thought Aunt Mira was your mother. We let you think that to spare you pain. You were an abandoned child. Life was unjust from the start. You liked your Aunt Mira and wished to think she was your mother so we did nothing to dissuade you. We also feared that if you knew who your real mother was you could not bear it. You were too young. Now you are grown up. I told your aunt and uncle two or three years ago it was time to let you know the truth.

'Three million? Take care of it now!'

But they said it is unwise to tell the truth and expose a noble lie. I do not think so. I believe the truth will come to light eventually. Right now you are abroad with a brave new future before you. It is probably easier for you to accept historical misfortune.

'Fuck that! Go get him!'

Lan, I must tell you …

'You heard me. Get on it! Don't waste time!'

Your real mother is Lulu in the corner apartment …

'Don't give me that shit!'

Yes, she is the one. You would not think to look at her now but she was beautiful and intelligent once. She was her family's only child. Her parents were old-fashioned intellectuals. How could they ever accept an illegitimate child? They hid her out with relatives in the city to avoid gossip and arranged to have her deliver you in a hospital downtown. Your Aunt Mira and Lulu were good friends back then. When Mira learned that Lulu's family would abandon you she told your aunt and uncle—my parents—who always wanted a healthy child to take care of them in old age. They made a secret pact with Lulu's parents and took you home. Lulu's family said you were a posthumous child. They said your father was killed in the gang war of 1976. I do not know much about it. I just heard two gangs in the twenty-four buildings fought about something connected with crickets and a lot of kids died. But Lulu told Mira your father was not killed. He was not even in the gang war. She said he was a student at the worker-peasant-soldier university and a Party member. She said he never knew about you. She refused to say who he was; she probably wanted to protect him. She was too kind.

Lan, I try my best to imagine how you must feel now. But I know that no matter how hard I try my feelings could never be like yours. Maybe I take revenge on you subconsciously—maybe I want you to suffer as I did. But I trust you will get over it and be stronger for having had the experience. Truth is not always beautiful or good but in the face of truth we are forever humble.

A loud pop startles me.

We have no clue to your father's identity except an old book—a Qing dynasty cricket manual. Lulu gave it to Mira for safekeeping and said your father would claim it one day. We felt strange: How could a Party member own a feudal relic like that? Your aunt and uncle were scared and almost threw it away. But when the Gang of Four was arrested they hid it and hoped to stay out of trouble. Your father never showed up. Maybe Lulu had no chance to tell him where it was. Ever since her parents discovered she was pregnant they kept her sequestered. And soon after your birth she grew incoherent. She got worse and worse—you saw how she was. Your aunt has the book ...

The letter is snatched away and replaced by a glass of champagne—bubbles rise cheerfully.

I look up.

'Don't you know me?' He grins. 'Come see the fireworks.'

He puts a coat over my shoulders and escorts me out back.

The air is icy. The champagne glass chills my fingers.

'Ten! Nine! Eight! Seven! …' I hear shouts from Red Regime.

He holds me close.

Skyrockets flare and shriek on takeoff. I see only blurred colors and lights.

The wind carries raucous drunken song: 'Should auld acquaintance be forgot, and never brought to mind? …'

He nuzzles my ear and whispers, 'Happy New Year.'

(The End)

Author's Note

This translation aims to capture in idiomatic English the exact contextual meaning of a novel written in idiomatic Chinese. To capture that meaning it must often rephrase the text, which rendered word for word would be a Chinglish travesty. To further ease reader access, some background may help.

The leitmotif and clue to the mystery is cricket fighting, which dates back to the eighth-century Tang dynasty (618–907 C.E.) acme. Begun as an imperial court amusement, cricket fighting became a popular obsession like bullfighting in Spain or cockfighting in Southeast Asia and survived underground during the Cultural Revolution (1966–1976) when traditional art and entertainment were repressed as feudal relics. Revived during the 1980s, it thrives now—raising crickets for sale is big business; so is gambling on cricket fights despite illegality.

The plot involves two families—the narrator's and her nanny's—but includes satellite characters. Nicknames typical of the 1970s and 1980s reflect social reality at the time and are convenient for non-Chinese readers today.

Narrator's Family
Lan, main character and narrator
Aunt, her foster mother Mrs. Yang
Uncle, her foster father Mr. Yang
Cousin aka **Cripple**, their daughter (presumed dead)
Mira, aunt's younger sister (deceased)
Grandmother, aunt's mother (deceased)

Nanny's Family

Nanny, Mrs. Yu (deceased)

Wizard, cricket cognoscente Mr. Yu

Jianguo, their older son (deceased)

Jianhua, their daughter

Jianjun aka **Boss Yu**, their younger son

Jin Zhilong aka **Brother Jin** aka **Big Boss**, Jianhua's husband and Lan's employer

Ting, Jianhua and Brother Jin's daughter

Grandmother aka **Granny Lump**, Wizard's mother (deceased)

Other Characters

Ray, American journalist and Lan's lover

Linda, Ray's colleague

Amy, Lan's colleague

Nancy, Lan's colleague

Jason aka **Little Boss**, Lan's supervisor

Liang Zengqi aka **Master Liang**, cricket-fight organizer

South-of-Yangtze Number-One Handler, cricket-fighting master

Loony Lulu, harmless lunatic in Lan's old neighborhood

Blind, teenage boy in the Celestial Dragons gang there (deceased)

Commander, Celestial Dragons gang leader (deceased)

Howitzer, Wild Fires gang leader (deceased)

General Guan, red cricket named after Han dynasty (206 B.C.E.–220 C.E.) war hero Guan Yu (160–219 C.E.) deified four centuries postmortem and still worshipped today

Political Terms

Resist-Japan War, World War II (1937–1945)

Liberation War, Civil War (1946–1949)

Resist-America Aid-Korea War, Korean War (1950–1953)

Great Leap Forward famine (1958–1962) due to communization of farming and forced grain procurement in the government's drive to Communism (1958–1960)—tens of millions died

Cultural Revolution (1966–1976) from its proclamation to the Gang of Four purge a month after Mao died

For more information or to receive our newsletter, please contact us at: info@worldeditions.org.